FATE OF THE

Julius Ocwinyo

FOUNTAIN PUBLISHERS
Kampala

Fountain Publishers
P.O. Box 488
Kampala
E-mail: sales@fountainpublishers.co.ug
           publishing@fountainpublishers.co.ug
Website:www.fountainpublishers.co.ug

Distributed in Europe and Commonwealth countries outside Africa by:
African Books Collective Ltd,
P.O. Box 721,
Oxford OX1 9EN, UK.
Tel/Fax: +44(0) 1869 349110
E-mail: orders@africanbookscollective.com
Website: www.africanbookscollective.com

Distributed in North America by:
Michigan State University Press
1405 South Harrison Road
25 Manly Miles Building
East Lansing, MI 48823-5245
E-mail: msupress@msu.edu
Website: www.msupress.msu.edu

ISBN 978 9970-02-101-7

Dedication

To Francis Odongo-Achanga
and Richard Opeto-Wonruku
Who should know why.

Fate of the Banished

It was all a matter of choice between knowing and unknowing. And Satan craftily hastened to point them in the direction they both craved, and offered them the delicious apple. They partook of the crisp and juicy fruit and that marked a point of no return for them. The Lord banished them from the Garden of Eden and thus their fate was sealed. They and their children and their children's children down to the umpteenth generation would henceforth be subject to afflictions and temptations and flaws they had hitherto not known – pain and disease and pestilence; labour and war and death; theft and duplicity and fornication and adultery and murder, and the undying hunger for something better. And no single descendant of that first couple would be exempt, for we had lost all that was good and gentle and beauteous upon that day of our banishment.

No reference is made in this book to any person living or dead, or to any specific historical fact. If any similarity exists between one or other of the characters in the fiction and any individual, past or present, or between an episode in the story and a historical occurrence, then such similarity should be treated as purely accidental.

J.O.
1997

I

The priest lay on the bed, spreadeagled on his back. Dark-red blood from his punctured heart had oozed down his narrow chest and over the plateau of his belly. The blood had congealed and stuck in his pubic hair as it had flowed down between his legs, carefully skirting his shrivelled manhood now flaked gray with the woman's dried wetness. The woman herself, huddled up like a foetus, was lying naked on her side in a gelling pool of her own blood, her face grotesquely pressed into the cold glazed cement, her hands gripped vice-like between her thighs as if even in death she was still trying to shield Eve's shame.

The crowd had gathered like a swarm of flies around the dead bodies. While some clucked their sympathy and pity, others, especially the women and the more mature girls, wept openly over this one shameless act on the part of one of their own species. They were deeply outraged, angrily wondering what was wrong with some married women? Couldn't she have paddled her itch elsewhere, far away from where she lived, for somebody else to do the scratching for her? Now look how she'd gone and bungled it all! Mothers who had urged their daughters to try and ensnare the priest were angrier still, viewing the dead woman's success with the padre as betrayal of their daughters' best interests.

The men, on their part, were deeply shocked, for this was something they had least expected to happen. As the Chairman of the local Parish Council said, he didn't even suspect the dead priest to have been capable of what he had done: to go sleeping with people's wives, of all things! Who, he asked, had not said – after the priest had been with them for about two years – ah! now we have at last been sent someone who is a living embodiment of what he preaches!

The priest, having only just returned from a four-year course in Church History at the Gregorian University in Italy, had proven beyond dispute that a man could live celibate yet unperverted if he knew how to go about sublimating his no doubt overpowering

1

sexual energies, how to direct their surging force into less scandalous channels. So from the day after his arrival, routinely, he had jogged himself to exhaustion every other evening, modestly taking the least frequented paths in the village, never wanting to give the local people the impression he was doing this jogging to show off.

After bathing, he would resume the work of ministering to his flock. He would visit them in their homes to advise them upon this or that matter, holding family prayers with them, chatting with them about ordinary things over a saucer of roast groundnuts or simsim, or a cup of oversweet tea. He loved them, and that in turn inspired in them a deep love and respect for him.

At night, young as he was, he found the temptation to fill the empty space beside him on his wooden bed easy to overcome. He was a great lover of books. He especially loved those books that explored in depth the wellsprings of human attitudes and actions. Consequently, his library consisted not only of works on theology and philosophy and Church history, but also such serious fiction as Iris Murdoch's *The Bell,* Wole Soyinka's *The Interpreters,* as well as *The Shoe of the Fisherman* and a Faulkner or two. He also had an abiding love for geography, though his interest mainly centred on the two dozen well-thumbed *National Geographics* which he kept in a cardboard box at the head of his bed, so he could dip into it whenever the urge to read about volcanoes or earthquakes or the early civilisation of the Incas seized him.

Not everyone approved of the priest's conduct, though. Some couldn't help openly wondering what kind of man he was that he shouldn't occasionally break his vow and have a little fun with some of those unmarried girls who seemed to adore him so much - as any normal warm-blooded young man would. Or was he – God forbid – one of those unfortunate men whose prod did not stand up? Despite the utterances of his detractors, some of which reached his ears, all had gone well for about two years.

Suddenly, however, when everybody, Catholic and non-Catholic, Christian and non-Christian alike, had begun to think him invulnerable to a woman's charms, his carefully-constructed castle of pastoral self-preservation had simply crumbled.

Father Santo Dila – the local people fondly called him simply *Padi,* the vernacular corruption of the Italian *Padre,* blew on his flute, once again offering the note that the choir had got wrong.

'Now breathe in-out, in-out. Yes, that's good. Now clear your throats.' He cleared his own throat. 'Are you ready now?' The choir nodded in unison. He blew on the flute again. 'O.K., one, two, three begin!'

Padi's arms flailed away, a flute-surmounted vibrancy of hymnal ecstasy, as the choir launched into a rather complicated hymn the father had himself composed while still in Rome. As usual, the women sang with keener interest, and with greater abandon than the men, giving fully of themselves in this prelude to the soul-stirring performance they put up in church every Sunday.

If father Dila were asked why he insisted that choir practice take place virtually every other day, he would have said, and truthfully enough, that that was the only way to keep the church choir in peak form.

'There's somebody still singing off-key,' said the padre. 'Yes, you there! I've caught you at last! By the way, I almost always forget your name.'

And the girl – it was difficult to think of her as a woman: something about her manner, her entire disposition, obliged the priest to always conceive of her as a girl – said, 'Flo, Flo's the name.'

'Yes, Flo, you're not singing very well.'

Flo giggles, tinkle-like, and says: 'Look, *Padi,* the problem is perhaps that I'm too far away. Can I stand next to you so that I can hear you sing better?'

Her tone is bantering, of course, but urges acquiescence. Her mates rustle with laughter.

'It's all right, it's perfectly all right,' says *Padi.* 'Come right over.'

Flo plants herself next to the priest and her singing suddenly improves. She no longer gropes uncertainly for the more difficult notes but plucks them out, holding them firmly like someone who has found her musical fingers at last.

'Ah there, that is beautiful! Could we try it again?'

Another trial on the flute, and another heady trip into ecstasy.

In essence, father Dila would have been telling the truth, insisting that he regularly called choir practice because he didn't want the performance of his choir to sag, because he wanted to keep them on their musical toes. Of course, he did *know* that some members of the Church choir had ulterior motives. He had more than once caught a few of them exchanging meaningful glances, or swapping velvet-soft smiles, but that had not discouraged him at all. If some of them wanted to turn their mates into lovers – especially those of them who were still single – well, what right had he to stop them even if he could? In any case, he himself obtained his own legitimate satisfaction from listening to those feminine voices, drinking in their various timbres like a wind sock, the harmony of the voices thrilling him, soaking deep into his bones, soothing him. But surely such a thrill constituted the joy one should derive from seeing one's efforts at musical stewardship rewarded with such splendid singing, and there was nothing improper in that!

'Now, I think that's enough for today. Shall we say a little prayer before we disperse?'

They all knelt down, humble supplicants in this open-air cathedral, the girl-woman still beside him, her presence palpable and pungent and heady like onion. He led them in a brief prayer until the final 'Amen' and then, as was his wont, courteously hung around for a little chat before they could drift back to their homes. Flo was in the last group to leave, one man and three women, and she insisted on wishing the priest an emphatic 'good night, see you next time' before departing. He sensed something nebulous and rather formless but didn't allow the nascent impression to take root.

* * *

'The sods are after us, let's run for it!' Apire said, grabbing his AK47 sub-machine gun and dashing for a nearby septic tank. The tank was on the premises of a newly-constructed Lepers Home on which work had been completed just before the outbreak of the war. It had not had the chance to be used. Apire leapt into the tank, closely followed by Erabu, another fighter, only 18. The cause of the flight was the faint chugging of a distant gunship.

'D'you think here we're safe enough?' asked Apire.

'How can I tell? I've been in this thing no more than a month, and had it not been for you the damn machine would have caught me still resting on my bum,' Erabu giggled nervously.

'Your mother should be really worried. Does she know you're with us?'

'Yes, 1 told her before 1 left home.' A look of pride suffused Erabu's face before he added, sadly, 'Home, of course, meant the camp for displaced people where we'd been temporarily settled.'

'She didn't ask the reason why you should have decided to take up arms?'

'No she didn't, but I think she understood, the way women usually understand such things. Only, the poor woman was so scared for me that she threatened to curse me if I took so much as a step into the bush.'

'And you came away just the same?'

'I told her it wouldn't make much difference to me whether she cursed or not. I'd still leave.'

'The old woman must have wept herself sick.'

'Don't know.'

Fear! The cold, clammy slugbelly of fear slimming its way down Erabu's back as the chugging of the gunship got closer and closer and became an eerie whining roar as the machine came in low, the whirl of its rotors flattening the grass and sending loose pebbles skittering God knows where. Stomach-loosening fear as it looped round and came back suspicious, flying slower and lower still in all its prehistoric hideousness, its stout wheels almost skimming the tops of the short trees. Bladder-clenching fear as silence suddenly descended, a cold, stuffy silence, suspect in its utter deathlikeness. Fear easing out as the minutes ticked by and the ears became receptive to those infinitesimal sounds of God's tiny creatures, the cockroach scudding rustlingly on the concrete wall of the septic tank, or the grasshopper up around the rim of the tank going *thwak-thwak-thwak-thwak* in amorous invitation to a loved one. Sounds other than the thumping of one's own heart or the whistle of one's own breath through the nostrils.

'Does it always have to be this way?' Erabu asked, beginning to relax at last.

'Which way?' Apire seemed absent-minded, far away.

'Feeling walled-in, with nowhere to escape to, and wanting to wet your pants, or even crap in them?'

'What did you expect?' Apire asked and gave a brief laugh, brief, and cold and low.

'Oh dear, but that machine is ugly!'

'Which machine?'

'The helicopter. Looks like a monster in a nightmare.'

And the whole damn business of war is an unrelieved nightmare, Apire thought, and some of the things he had witnessed in this war passed before his eyes, kaleidoscopic. Especially one particular episode his memory kept dredging up from his subconscious where it lay coiled like a waiting mamba. It came during his waking hours and occasionally in nightmares when he was asleep. It would sneak up on him, coldly, relentlessly, even when he was sleeping drunk and stuporous beside his wife on those rare occasions when he felt the coast was clear and slipped away to have a few days of lethargic respite in his maternal uncle's home where he had asked her to go for 'safekeeping'. Nobody there knew he was a fighter. They believed he was a wayward fisherman who vanished from home for weeks, sometimes months at a time. Oh what an irresponsible husband he was! No wonder his wife looked so sad!

This nightmare came back now in all its horror and ugliness... They had attacked an Army detach and driven the soldiers away, killing some in the process. After lugging all the undamaged weaponry and some of the captured provisions to their own base camp, they had agreed that that day's victory was something worth celebrating with roast goat's meat and drinking and dancing. So they had slaughtered two of the goats they had bought for that purpose. They always bought their food, thus also buying the goodwill of the people among whom they circulated, bought it with money they seized, violently, from people they considered to be their enemies.

They had cut up the goat's meat and skewered it on sticks and placed the sticks over numerous slow fires and allowed the meat to roast slowly, sizzling appetizingly, its pungent smell lazily spreading around the forest where they had pitched camp and wailing heavenward. They had drunk strong 'manly' liquor straight from jerrycans and smoked cigarettes and marijuana. They had sung, yes they had sung in a medley of tenors and rich baritones, throwing caution to the winds. He had danced until his dance partner, a comrade he loved and respected, the only real friend he had had at that time, with whom he had joined up on the same day - they had danced until the head of this dear friend and comrade had exploded into a loose mass of gory tissue and bone, just like a small, dark, flickering cloud, as he, Apire, stood there uncomprehending. One shard of skull, floating almost in slow motion, had come his way and planted itself on his mouth like a seal. His hand had gone up to brush off the soggy saucer of bone. The stodgy goo clung to his fingers; and as he smelt blood and flesh and saw his friend tumbling backwards ever so slowly he, comprehending at last, had found himself lifting one leaden foot after another in a parody of a run. He could swear to God he had heard nothing, not a single gunshot!

Yet he had survived, he'd survived with his gun intact. He had crashed wildly through the forest, which a moment before had been full of song and laughter but was now shot through with cracking pinpoints of light and echoing explosions. Of those in that forest camp only about thirty – roughly half their original strength – had survived.

Then delayed shock had set in and he had retched and vomited floods of meat-laden booze, fetching it up from deep within himself, his bowels heaving, almost wrenching away from their moorings...

'I'm saying, can we get out of this rat-hole now?' enquired Erabu.

'Sorry, didn't quite catch that.'

'I could see your thoughts had gone wandering again.'

'Oh yes, yes, one really can't help it, can one?'

'Can we get out now?'

'Think so, but we need to be careful. I'll lead the way.'

* * *

Father Dila had lately become vaguely aware that the choir practice did something to him which no other activity did. It hadn't always been like that, not right from the moment he had begun to hold choir practice in that rural parish. Things had begun to happen to him only a few months ago and he had failed to trace their source. No, it wasn't only the soft breeziness of those female voices stroking the nap of his ruffled emotions in great soothing sweeps; it was something else, something insidious, nebulous yet strong, intractable. If he had been watching his congregation closely enough, he would have noticed that some of them prayed and sang with a devotion to him which was stunning - and which should have been deeply disconcerting to him. But *Padi*, having the kind of temperament that didn't need to be brought into line with the canons and exigencies of his calling every now and then, and being rather of a shy disposition, did not at all realise that his presence at the altar caused quite a stir among the female members of his flock. A flutter barely noticeable, yet perceptible to the finely-tuned senses of some of the male congregation many of whom, believing the priest was fully conscious of what he caused to happen among those women, admired and respected him all the more for his moral strength. A few of them, of course, wondered why he shouldn't take advantage of them, especially the girls, since man eateth where he worketh and no one would object to a herdsman partaking of milk from the cows he looks after.

So the priest had been unaware – until this moment in the confessional box. The moment Flo knelt down on the other side of the dividing screen, his thoughts went back to the time he'd picked Flo out as the culprit when his beautiful hymn had been mis-sung, when he'd pointed at her and said 'you there'. Somehow, for whatever reason, that minor incident kept surging back to the surface of his memory, demanding attention.

Now Flo crosses herself and says the requisite prayer preceding the confession of sins, then proceeds to confess. All minor sins but many of them of course. She stops, looks deep in the eyes of the priest, a strange longing luminescent in the depths of her own eyes. She coughs, spluttering.

'Yes Flo, have you finished?' asks *Padi*, wondering.

'Yes, *Padi*,' answers Flo, virtually inaudible.

'Now go and say the 'Hail Mary' twenty times.'

Still Flo hasn't risen to leave. She stares at him, eyes mellow, then suddenly dissolving in two soft pools of water. Tears, oh God she's shedding tears! What have I done to evoke such a strong reaction? But I've only instructed her to say the 'Hail Mary' a few times!

'What's wrong, what's wrong Flo?' the priest, frantic, flustered looks left then right through the fine-mesh wire screening off the confessional, snatches a look behind him. No one. Thank goodness there's nobody lounging around the confessional box to witness this little drama!.

'...you.'

Flo has said something which he has missed, whatever the wellspring of her secret sorrow is.

'You said something?'

'Yes, *Padi*, ... I know it's not proper telling you this, but I'm – ahem – I don't sleep these days for thinking about you – I love you, *Padi*, I really do.'

Flo gets up groggily, steadies herself and shuffles bashfully away, without waiting for the service to begin.

A maelstrom of conflicting emotions assails the padre, buffeting him with their overwhelming force. He clamps his temples with his palms, making a tremendous effort to think ... draws a blank ... head a bundle of nylon-strings tugging at the thought-centre, tangled skeins tightening around the core of the brain, bunching it up, scattering it in a hundred and one amber pinpoints of light that flash momentarily in front of his eyes, vanishing briefly, only to return with greater intensity ... head throbbing, throbbing, throbbing, surging into clopping of the church drums outside till drums and brain are entwined in that one intimacy of throbbing pain, blinding him with the whole of his being dissolving in the pulsating weightlessness of a choking darkness.

When *Padi* finally opens his eyes, his head is an appendage

fashioned out of onion-skin and housing a cheeky imp clanging away at a little empty tin.

He excuses himself to the Chief Catechist, 'Oh you see - ahem – I've suddenly developed a blinding headache – ahem – my usual migraine – ahem – could you stand in for me today, only today?' And he hurries away in a great flurry of leg-churned cassock, leaving the catechist wondering agape: Since when did the priest have bouts of migraine?

II

'Chase him! Cattle-thief! Run! Catch him! Ruuun!' A great hubbub
had risen from the throats of a multitude of hysterical humanity, a
mass of shared frustrations, frustrations sharp and bitter as the pulp
of immature gourd. The crowd came running in a body, anxious
to mete out instant justice, blind justice, to this intrepid scoundrel,
this piece of thieving scum, symbol of all the hurt and humiliation
they had suffered at the hands of cattle-rustlers.

They ran in a solid body of multicoloured humanity, intent on
the capture of this one man. They ran slipping, stumbling, falling,
getting up, staggering, shouting, falling, leaping up - they ran with
eyes arrowed on the fleeing back of the young man, the little thief,
so light of foot; he seemed to float on the little puffs of dust he
raised with each footfall, scudding, desperately running, seeking
sanctuary from the collective wrath of his rapidly closing pursuers,
flying, leaping!

Then the thief stumbled, slipped and fell, his gun flying from
his grip, landing clattering in the middle of the narrow cattle-track.
Instantly the crowd were upon him, pummelling, kicking, clubbing,
scratching for what seemed a decade to the thief, until somebody
came up with a better method of lynching him: he should first be
tried, and then punished.

The 'judge', selected more because of his intimidating appearance
than for anything else, sat down under a tree, a huge shaggy man
with taut sinews and not a single ounce of fat on him, big and jet-
black and ominous, with a small head and little, red pig-like eyes.
He squinted at the thief standing before him, bloodied and with
hands roped behind his back – nobody quite knew where the rope
had appeared from – and a few feet of the rope held slack by a short,
thickset man who stood behind him.

Then the 'interrogation' began.

Judge: 'You know what we are going to do to you?'

Thief: 'No.'

Jeers rose up from the crowd, in unison, like a cloud of flies from a mound of rotting mangoes.

Judge (taking a long look at the thief, coolly): 'We are going to kill you."

'Kill him, kill him!' a hundred thunderous Judaeans clamouring for blood, casting a blanket vote of condemnation, obviating personal responsibility.

Thief: 'If you have to kill me, please allow me to explain first, let me explain.'

The judge looks at his unsworn jury, gets their buzzing approbation for the thought - the one single thought - writ large on his face.

Judge: 'No, we are going to kill you, but we haven't yet decided how.'

Thief (desperate): 'Please spare my life, I'm no thief ...'

Another flight of jeers from the crowd and an accompanying volley of stones converge on the thief's body. They are hurled more to underscore the crowd's contempt than to cause bodily harm.

Judge (immensely pleased with himself): 'Anybody with a suggestion as to how to kill this thief? We hang him?'

'Yes, hang him, hang him!'

And one voice proffers a method which is a fairly sophisticated variation on the hanging theme.

'Yes we hang him,' says the voice, 'but not by the neck.' He looks pleased, deliriously happy. 'We hang him by the feet and then roast him alive.'

A great roar of support rises from the crowd, muffling the thief's 'no-no-no-no's' of protest.

Thief: 'Please spare my life, just this once and I won't come to these parts again, please!'

'Shut up!' a thunderous snapping command from the multitude as the thief now blubbers meaninglessly, wetting his trousers in the process.

'We hang the fool over a fire,' insists the voice, 'a very slow fire remember, until he dies. I guess that'll teach him a lesson he'll remember long afterwards,' he concludes, and spits.

As if controlled by a single master brain, the crowd scatters to collect faggots, some dry, some still rather wet, faggots which they place at the exact spot where the 'judge' has been sitting in sadistic wisdom just a few moments before.

In a flash the cattle thief is felled and hobbed with a long rope around the ankles and one end of the rope is flung up over a branch and the man run up the tree like a flag up a flagpole.

A score of men excitedly pull, too many men for such a slip of a man, as he rises up the tree with a thick, rough bole, a tree in full leaf, an *olam* tree. And the poor man yelling all the time, 'Please save me somebody, I did not steal anything, never have I stolen anything in my life, take the gun – take everything but let me go, spare my life!' And the crowd jeer all the more and laugh gustily and some spit directly into the man's eyes as he dangles in mid-air with his arms flailing without hope, the hands frantically groping for a hold; and the thief is yelling all the time, and he gives vent to a big anal explosion and his pants convulse suspiciously where the explosion has occurred. The crowd cheer uproariously and some of them comment: 'He smells, Lord how he stinks!'

Then the fire is started and it is not permitted to burn fiercely, the thief kicking and straining to free himself as blood begins to flow freely from his nose, at first tear-drops of cherry melding with the fire below, then turning into a double-barrelled flood.

Many moments later, the eyes heave out of their sockets and explode, sending up a further cheer among the audience. Apire, beside himself with excitement, picks up a club and smashes the moribund head into a soggy mass.

The thief is then taken down from the *olam* tree and leant against its thick bole, away from the fire, and an order goes out from the 'judge' that the murdered man shouldn't be buried. People go there to see him - men and women, young and old, even children – all go there to see this strange man, this dead cattle thief with the smashed head. They go to that same spot day after day the way you would go to watch some freak animal born to a normal mother; they go there as if to find out how the corpse is faring...

Now the man, badly wasted, sinews clinging precariously to yellowed bones, is walking towards Apire, blindly, groping his way, bones clattering like an assemblage of dry sticks; groping, seeking with fingers, skin dried taut over the bones, all joints, groping, searching with nails gone black with rot for Apire's eyes, hell-bent on gouging them out. Apire cringes, his back against a tough irresistibility of membrane, buffalo hide of absymal darkness, frantically trying to push away the dessicated fingers, even as the musty smell of earthly putrefaction assails his nose and the pained groaning from the gnashing teeth reaches his ears. The skeletal fingers, cold and mouldy with death, touch his eyelids, in a sort of suspended contact, hovering, still undecided as to which exact spot to drive in their pointed lethality...

A cold hand gripped Apire's aim like a tourniquet and he woke up bawling, sitting up instantly.

'Shut up! What the hell d'you think you're doing bellowing like that?'

'Oh did I shout? I was only dreaming.'

"Did you shout indeed! You bellowed loud enough to wake up all the sleeping ghosts.'

'Where's my gun?'

'It's right here with me – what was the dream about?'

'Well, something we did at the beginning of this war. We caught a cattle-thief, strung him up on a tree branch, feet-first, and roasted him alive, slowly.'

'Roasted him alive? Oh dear!' and Erabu wondered what it could be like roasting a man alive, whether it would thrill or disgust, that pungent-smell from the mixed grill of human muscle and hair and gristle and bone and blood. 'Must have been a horrible experience.'

'For whom?'

'For you. For the man.'

'I enjoyed it at the time. Now I wonder why I helped with the poor man's murder at all. No, I don't mean feeling bad about killing him. But I'm pretty fed up with this never-ending nightmare.'

'Stop thinking about him.'

'I don't even think about him. But the dream keeps coming back. Again and again and again.'

'His spirit is haunting you.'

'Perhaps. Perhaps I should go home and be cleansed. I can easily acquire a black sheep. But why on earth should it be him and nobody else? Of all the people I've killed?'

'He has a stronger head, that's what my people would say.'

'It wasn't strong enough to stand up to that club anyhow,' remarked Apire, wryly wondering what turns a man in his twenties into a vicious murderer?

He hadn't been one to frequently turn his thoughts inward upon himself, but the war had made him introspective, thinking about the whys and wherefores of his thoughts and actions and reactions and dreams like a damned philosopher. While still in secondary school, he had heard about a bunch of fools called philosophers who lived purely in their heads and eternally sat planted under trees like Buddha to puzzle out the mysteries of life. He had been told there was one called Plato and another, Socrates – the greatest, it seemed, of the lot. And the most foolish. Why agree to imbibe a whole cupful of some foul-tasting and lethal liquid just to persuade your detractors that your ideas are a damn sight better than theirs? Die in defence of ideas? That was the height of stupidity! Now, that Socrates fellow would have driven his point home better by slashing a few of those Greek necks with a panga or whatever weapon they used in those lands!

That brought him up short. Why did he always have to think thoughts of death? Could it be because his father's murdered body had been desecrated so ignobly?

* * *

A slap, sharp and stinging, to his mother's cheeks. 'You're going to tell us where your husband is or else ...' gesture with the index finger across the throat. 'And it won't be only you, but all your children as well. After we've got a little fun out of you – in the presence of those children.'

His mother had whined like a whelp and delicately fingered the slapped spot. Then she had said something inaudible. The man had shone a torch directly into her eyes and asked her again where her husband was, without slapping her this time. Then he had switched on the bedroom light.

The men – he had later realised they had been five in all – had crashed in at midnight when they had all been in bed. The three he had had a chance to set eyes on were all young, must have been in their twenties and thirties, but to his child's eyes they looked a lot older.

He had been ten, going on eleven.

They had pretended complete unawareness of his presence at first – his presence as well as that of his two brothers, Acaye and Matto, and his sister Betty. Betty, who was on vacation from secondary school, would have been around sixteen at that time; she was beautiful, very beautiful in an innocent, nubile, yet incomplete way; and she had been the first among the children to attract the attention of the man who had slapped their mother. He had stooped and peeled back the two blankets they shared, one between each pair of them. He had peeled them back like a pair of very loose banana skins and had left them naked except for the sister who was wearing a petticoat. They had been cowering under the blankets, pressing themselves against each other and into the two thin foam mattresses overlaid with plastic sheeting, hoping against hope that a hole would appear in the cement floor and swallow them up. The man had chuckled deep in his scraggy throat, delightedly, and had turned over each one of them, firmly but gently, onto their backs, starting with him, Apire, and ending with Betty. He had used the thick toe of his platform shoe. They had offered no resistance, hypnotised by fear, rolling over easily, and Apire had noticed, uncomprehending yet full of dread, the front of the man's trousers heave and bunch as he ran his amused eyes over the inert body of their sister.

They had watched as he pulled her up, jerked her up in fact, and pushed her none too gently to stand beside her mother. Then he had proceeded to kick the boys howling onto their feet and shown them into a corner of the fairly large bedroom.

'Now you're two - that means all five of us can be comfortably accommodated,' the minion of State Security had addressed their mother and sister. 'You know, a little light entertainment in the line of duty,' an amused wink in the direction of the boys, 'while the boys watch the show.'

Both mother and daughter had begun to weep, big tears welling up in their eyes and rolling down their cheeks like pear-shaped marbles. Their shoulders had rocked as their bodies convulsed to great, silent sobs, Betty with arms entwined across her orange-sized breasts, trying as best she could to hide their tempting nudity.

'Your husband isn't here in this bedroom, Maria.' Where had he learnt the name? Apire tried to figure this out. 'That means he hasn't been sleeping here, next to you. Otherwise these children wouldn't be sharing the bedroom with you when the sitting room is large enough to take four sleeping children and more. Unless, of course, you don't mind doing it within earshot of the children.' Doing what? Apire had wondered; this man seems to be saying lots of things with hidden meanings! Yet his mother had looked deeply embarrassed and pained. 'Now, for the last time, tell me where he's hiding, will you?' No response. 'Well, I think I should give you time to think, exactly five minutes. And do not make any attempt to escape through the window because it is covered. You'll only end up getting a bullet kissing your beautiful belly button.'

He had chortled and gone out swaggering, a revolver held nonchalantly in his left hand and his dark glasses in his right, and had locked them in the bedroom.

Muted sounds of speech, voices belonging to about three people, a buzz of conversation swelling and subsiding like a sinister tide. A rip, then a long tearing sound of fabric. A series of thuds, followed by a splintering crash. Dead silence, but only for a few seconds. Heavy tread of platformed footsteps heading towards the bedroom door, clic of key in mortice lock, then the door is flung violently open by another pistol-toting protector of the State in all his bell-bottomed, T-shirted splendour.

'All of you, out of here and into the sitting room, quick!'

Orders are orders, so they had stampeded into the bright-lit sitting room, State Security trudging along behind them like an evil spirit.

'Now I'll teach you the importance of telling the truth.' He had turned to his comrades. 'Hey, *Wandugu,* let's have these people do a little singing for us, shall we?'

An avalanche of head-spinning blows and thudding kicks had descended upon them, with pistol butts and fists and platform shoes flailing away in a dizzying ferment of action. They had screamed and begged until they were all down on their hands and knees, but the men wouldn't stop, not even when Acaye, only six, had been stretched out unconscious.

'Now get up, you two!' This was directed at Maria and Betty, who rose up unsteadily, and kept on trembling with fear.

'You two are the oldest in this house and you should therefore know where Bruno is.' This from the man who had herded them out of the bedroom.

Apire wondered whether his mother or his sister had an inkling of where Bruno, their father, was. Acaye still lay unmoving on the cold floor.

'Now are you telling me where Bruno is? Or aren't you?' Angry flash of dark glasses brooding over flaring nostrils.

'We don't know, *afande,*' said mother and daughter in unison. *Afande's* eyes, inscrutable behind State-furnished hide-and-watch, had turned to the boys; 'You don't know either?'

'No!'

Frightened negation of hope of survival, as fear-constricted throats surrendered that 'no'.

'So you all don't know. That's very interesting.' *Afande* had moved slowly, nonchalantly, towards their mother. 'Now that you all don't know, we are going to replace him in this house. As father and husband.' He had handed his revolver to a comrade and reached out with both hands to grab Maria's dressing gown at her throat, ripping it open right down the front in a great rending sound of yielding fabric. *Afande* had then ambled over to Betty and eased down her half-slip, which had dropped in a pool of pink around her ankles. He had lifted her legs, one at a time, to sweep out first one portion, then another of the slip from under her. Then he had lifted the half-slip, gingerly, tested its consistency and texture with his fingers, sniffed it and flung it disdainfully into the middle of the room.

'I'm warning you,' he had told mother and daughter, 'when we finish with you, you won't be able to sit up or walk for several days. And after we've finished with you, we're going to complete the destruction of your household property. That tear in the sofa is only the beginning. Now, I happen to adore young girls, so you'll be the dish I taste first while Ali busies himself with your mother. And I prefer taking my women from behind, so you will please kneel down very obediently, because if you don't you'll get a kick where you'd least want it to strike.'

Afande had proceeded to place a large hand on Betty's shoulder and begun to push her gently down as the other hand started to loosen his broad belt.

A crash from somewhere up around the trap-door in the ceiling, then a thud, and a whirling bundle of axe-swinging fury had dented *Afande's* forehead with the blunt edge of the axe and had moved with incredible speed towards Ali who, mesmerised by this swirling apparition, had stood petrified with his arms up in a grotesque posture of prayer. Ali had received a fatal blow on the left temple and crumbled slowly to his knees before stretching out full-length on the floor, the blood pulsing out of the gash in his head like fluid from some spastic contraption.

Then all hell had broken loose as bullets had whipped over, behind and around them, thudding several times into Bruno and eventually felling him still clinging to the axe-handle in lifeless tenacity.

In the confusion Maria, Betty and Apire had managed to flee unscathed, leaving behind 13-year-old Matto dead from a bullet through the neck and another through the lung.

They had crashed noisily through the maize field in the back, then the cassava garden, colliding with standing stems and tripping over fallen ones, their bodies pain-racked knots of heart-thumping fright. They had spent the night in a swamp about three kilometres away from their home, cringing in the face of a vicious onslaught of squadrons of ravenous mosquitoes.

* * *

'Is your father still alive?' asked Apire.

'Oh yes, very much so. Why?' responded Erabu.

'Should every question be asked for a reason?'

'No, of course not, but it happens that you've that funny habit of asking very sudden questions, at times about things nobody else would be thinking of.'

And Erabu tried to puzzle out what made this young man tick, this close-faced, cryptic friend with the dreamy eyes, this comrade who would be present next to you, right there and vibrantly alive, yet would be very far away at the same time.

'...not there. Died when I was a kid.'

'Eh, what did you say?'

'My father. He died when I was still a kid. A State Security agent pumped him full with bullets after he'd clouted one agent unconscious and cut a gash in the head of another. The side of the head, and fatally. With an axe.'

'Oh.'

'They'd been five, those agents, and the three who'd not been hurt had rushed away their two unfortunate comrades in a Peugeot 504. One to hospital and the other to the mortuary.'

'Served them right!'

'They'd come back early in the morning the following day. In two cars - a Peugeot and a Fiat - and a lorry. Then they'd loaded the fridges - we had two - the TV and the electric cooker onto the lorry. After that, they'd proceeded to mutilate my father. Slashing rings around his arms so that he looked like some strange animal with all those angry gashes on his limbs. Plucking out the eyes and putting them in his palms. But that wasn't the worst part of it.'

'The brutes!' Erabu spat it out.

'Yes, those men were brutes. They sliced off his genitals - scrotum and all - crushed his balls and stuffed the whole lot into his tongueless mouth.'

'Where had the tongue gone?'

'It had been cut out. Now it was planted tip-first where the genitals had been.'

'My God!'

'Surprisingly they didn't do anything funny to my two brothers.'

'They'd killed those ones too?'

'No, only one. Took a bullet in the neck and another in the lung. The other brother had been battered into a coma before that. The agents took them outside and laid them out in the backyard. Then they left. It was my father who was locked inside the house, left to rot in there like a tramp.'

'Oh dear, and the boys?'

'Courageous neighbours took them away, to bury the one and have the other treated in a private hospital. They even took up a collection to pay his medical bill.'

'Your father never received a decent burial.' It was a statement not a question.

"The bones did, but after a long time. An armed guard was posted to watch the house until the body had fully decomposed.

After the guard had left, the same neighbours smashed in the doors and buried my father's bones in his home village. I had a glimpse of those bones without my mother noticing. They were in a cardboard box. Looking back, I realise that that was the moment I died.'

'Died?'

'I mean inwardly. A number of emotions became lost to me. Such as respect for most government institutions. Or love for much of humanity.'

Those lost emotions had been replaced by an overpowering, diffuse, unfocussed anger that he always tried to force down, but which kept rearing up like the multiple heads of some frightening snake he had been told about by his history teacher. Some myth that had to do with the ancient world of Rome. Or was it Greece? It didn't matter in any case. It was anger that swelled up as it was doing now, choking him, vicious anger that was tensile bunched-up cobra craving release.

Erabu sighed, thinking: no wonder he has such a faraway look in his eyes, those eyes that sometimes dull into a frightening dead-fish opacity.

'Is that why you're fighting this government? Because you do not respect government institutions?'

'Yes, most.'

'And if it was a government run by a different set of people, would you still fight it?'

'What does it matter that it's run by a different bunch of individuals? I'd still fight it if the opportunity presented itself.'

'You wouldn't discriminate? I mean between good government and bad government?'

'What's there to discriminate in favour of? And who would that help anyway?'

'Does this war help you?'

'Yes it does – in a way. To take the poison out of my system.'

'I see.' He, Erabu, had joined the insurgency for entirely different reasons.

III

Trouble had burst over Father Dila's head like a cluster bomb the Sunday Flo had told him in the confessional she couldn't sleep for love of him and he had hurried away flustered to the cloistered silence of the Mission House. The whole of that day he had stayed cooped up in his bedroom and done a lot of thinking. His brain had run riot, picking up one thought after another, taking a cold, hard look at them, rejecting them. He had completely lost appetite that day, so much was he troubled in spirit. He couldn't get down even a mouthful of the delicious sauce the old cook had prepared with such love and care.

The mission cook - worthy old woman - loved him like a son and pandered to his every gastronomic whim. She adored him and always brought him nice things from her home as if he were a little child who needed spoiling: honey with a little simsim paste stirred in, or white ants roasted and pounded and mixed with roast groundnuts pounded so finely that the paste dripped off your fingers and stuck to your gullet if you didn't swallow it with care, or homemade ghee which she always insisted should be kept in a covered earthenware bowl to fully bring out its hauntingly pungent flavour.

Much as he didn't want to disappoint the cook whom he loved as he would a mother, he couldn't get down anything that day, despite the poor woman's remonstrances, and her emotional pleading with him to drink only a little of the chicken broth, if only to make her happy. Suspecting that something more than the purported migraine was wrong with her 'son', she had put in an extra hour before knocking off.

What had first attracted him to that knock-kneed fellow called Ozoo, Father Dila couldn't understand. Ozoo wasn't his real name of course, but a nickname he had probably awarded himself following some escapade or other that he had brought off during his none-too-distant boyhood.

Ozoo had started out as an ordinary friend, then had quickly become a confidant and soon afterwards, his principal troubleshooter. Ozoo who didn't care a damn about what other people thought about him, who never allowed himself to be weighed down by the immensity of human problems. Ozoo whose insouciance and *joie de vivre* was only offset by the unflagging affection he had for his wife and children and the deep respect he accorded her. Ozoo whom you would never catch attending church but who brazenly visited him at the Mission House for a chat every now and then, even then making no secret of the fact that he didn't believe in that business of God having created man so that man would spend the whole of his life with his eyes turned skyward wondering whether he was making any impression on the Man Above. He was an unbeliever who didn't even try to rationalise his position - it just seemed so much a part of his irrepressibly optimistic nature. And he was a joy to have around. Perhaps one reason why Father Dila liked and respected Ozoo so much was that he was one of very few people who interacted with the padre on terms of equality, for he was frank and proud and hardly ever accepted anything for free, nor did he often ask for free things. Most of those 'devout' Catholics who came to 'chat' with him, on the other hand, usually made an attempt to flatter him in order to get something out of him.

The day after Flo's confession, the padre had sought out Ozoo to talk to him about this fresh crisis that had beset him. He had found Ozoo comfortably ensconced in a cane chair, happily imbibing a glass of *waragi* with two of his friends.

'Hello *Padi,* you're welcome, very much welcome and please do have a seat.' Ozoo had got up, beaming, vacating the cane chair for him. *Padi* had looked frantically around, picked up a twig and broken it in two. He had feared to look the three men straight in the face. Ozoo had been baffled.

'Hey, Padre, what's the matter? Aren't you going to sit down?

Father Dila had shaken his head and said, 'Look, Ozoo, I'd like to talk to you. I hope your companions won't mind missing you for few minutes.'

'Is it something confidential?'

'Yes, certainly.'

'Now you're going to make me miss my cherished booze.'

'Don't you worry, I'll buy you some when we're done talking.'

'Good, that's why I like you.'

Ozoo had enthusiastically grabbed Padi's hand and led him away.

'Now tell me what's worrying your intelligent head,' Ozoo had whispered. 'You look all done in like you didn't have a wink of sleep the whole of last night.'

'I didn't have any sleep at all, friend.' Then he had mumbled, 'restless is the body that wears the cassock.'

'What's that?'

'Oh, nothing very important really. I was only trying to speak like one of the books I once read in the Major Seminary.'

'Oh, I see,' said Ozoo, disappointed and suspecting the priest was trying to postpone the moment of revelation as much as possible. 'You still haven't told me what's troubling you.'

'You see, it's like this,' and he had launched into his narrative, telling him about what had happened at confession time the day before, not leaving out anything. When he had finished, Ozoo had laughed his thin, squeaky laughter that sounded more like a squeal of agony than an expression of mirth.

'Blind, blind, that's what you've been,' Ozoo had reminded him. 'Blind as a mole with your head burrowed in all those books. I've always caught you reading, as if you don't have anything better to do with your youth. Books and prayers all the time like those old Italian priests dragging out their last moments in arid retirement.'

'I hope you aren't condemning me?' The priest sounded disconsolate, hoping at least this one friend would understand his feelings and thoughts.

'No, not really. You see, *Padi*, everything has its own time. Books and prayers should be allotted their proper time. So should things like eating and sleeping. As well as the other needs - including the need to have fun at times.'

'I get enough fun from reading and listening to music, Ozoo.' The priest was suspicious, sensing that their conversation was veering towards a direction he least wanted it to take. 'Also from jogging.'

'And at night?' a little scorn had played around Ozoo's mouth, an expression of derision the *padre* would never have countenanced coming from someone else. 'What do you do with yourself at night? Exhaustion can't get rid of that primordial urge. Nor can dreams.'

'But I've tried, Ozoo. I've really tried to fulfil all the important obligations of my calling. Easily at first, but with increasing difficulty as time passed. I've had my moments of weakness and doubt, but they've been few and far between. And easy to overcome. Until yesterday.'

'Father, you still have a lot to learn. Wearing a *kanzu* and standing behind an altar or rubbing ash on people's foreheads isn't going to make you any more superhuman than I am. Especially since you're young, handsome and energetic. You're only punishing yourself trying to kill the sex urge.'

'What would you have done in my place?'

'I'd have reminded Flo that she's married and should therefore stop making a fool of herself. Then I'd have gone for one of the young unmarried women. Those who are in no danger of getting married since they're considered to be already too old for that.'

'And my flock would get to know about that and they'd say I'm no different from most of the rest of the clergy. You know as well as I do that we've earned ourselves a very bad reputation of late. The whole fraternity of the cloth. Remember my predecessor didn't spare any female thing that came near him, pinning them down one after another like a demented he-goat. And people breathed a big sigh of relief when he left. After several attempts had been made on his life.'

'He poached in all the wrong places.'

'Meaning?'

'Housewives, schoolgirls, catechumens. He never spared any of them. Keep clear of those and you're safe.'

'In giving way to temptation, I'd betray one of the most important tenets of my calling, Ozoo.'

'The problem with you, Father, is that you've been trained by too many white people for too long. And you've lived among white people for much too long.' Ozoo had sounded exasperated. 'Something – I don't know what – seems to have gouged out all the black stuffing in you and replaced it with white. But the sap kind of chose to remain black, and you're going to have to contend with that black sap in the pith of your being until the day you die, take it from me.' He had looked sternly at Father Dila. 'Anyway, I wouldn't be caught starving myself when there are lots of bright young things around who're simply dying to have a chance to hop into bed with me?'

'Even at the risk of getting people to think that the priesthood is just like any other job,' he had protested 'the only difference being that it's better paying than many jobs? And that you always have enough to eat and a car to drive around and a decent roof over your head?'

'Get those same people whose opinions you set such great store by into the Mission House and you'll see what they'll do. They'll run through the girls like a bushfire.'

'Perhaps.'

'Not perhaps, if the behaviour of your Chief Catechist is anything to go by.'

Father Dila had silently counted out a few banknotes, enough to buy a bottle of the crude gin, *waragi,* and thrust them into Ozoo's hand. Then he had bidden Ozoo goodbye.

Walking back to the Mission, the priest had winced in painful memory of the series of scandals the Chief Catechist had been involved in. His adulteries were so many you had to keep your ear constantly to the ground to keep abreast of them. In a kind of twisted way, he seemed to particularly relish housewives.

Then there were the numerous stories revolving around his sexual forays among the female mission workers as well as the older catechumens. His exploits were beginning to take on the dimensions of a legend. No wonder he had been dubbed *aryejali,* meaning 'chaser-after-married-women', yet carrying a connotation of awe and grudging respect for the often proud holder of the title. Father Dila had set traps for him in an effort to vindicate himself when he would fire the catechist, but the wily rogue had neatly sidestepped them all. Asking him point-blank to explain why people were saying what they were saying about him hadn't helped either, for he had a disarming way of dismissing the stories as simple "tongue-wagging by people who envy the house the old Italian priest built for me."

The catechist's wife, not wanting to be outdone, had also embarked on a campaign of her own, her principal targets apparently the many idle young men who seemed only too eager to take her to bed. Theirs was a broken family if ever there was one.

Yet, paradoxically, that he-goat of a catechist seemed to be quite popular with the local folks. Father Dila wondered whether he would ever be able to understand human nature at all.

* * *

Now the Father felt exactly like the adulterer he was, a modern day King David cuckolding an unsuspecting Uriah gone off to war, I though this had not detracted from the physical pleasure he had derived from the sin he had only just committed.

They lay side-by-side, satiated, the padre's right arm flung languorously across the waist of Flo who was lying on the wide wooden bed close to the oil-painted lower section of the wall. The walls always reminded Father Dila of a hospital, for their upper reaches were painted with yellow distemper and the lower part with old grey paint.

'I never thought I would do this kind of thing. At least not here and not with one of my parishioners,' said the priest.

'Are you feeling guilty?' Flo's eyes glinted with amusement.

'I don't know, I don't know yet. You know, guilt for me has at times been something I wouldn't feel immediately on commission of an act. Instead it would grow on me, slowly, eventually becoming overwhelming and assertive, pushing everything else into the background.'

I've allowed the intellectual in me to come out again, the Father thought wryly, catching the blank look he had become quite familiar with in Flo's eyes. Much as she was an intelligent girl, Flo had not had many years of schooling and thus at times completely failed to grasp some of the ideas he tried to express. Then he would spot that blankness descending over her eyes like nictitating membranes. That didn't bother him much, however, for whenever he felt an urge for philosophical discourse, there was always Ozoo, who could wax as philosophical as himself.

'I think I love you, Flo,' the Father said.

'That's strange, coming from a priest,' she chided gently.

'But I do. You know, up until that moment in the confessional never thought that I shared this weakness with the rest of mankind.' There you go again, Dila thought, talking like a damn philosopher. 'Well, I never thought I could fall in love with any woman.'

"H'm."

'Is that all you can say, h'm?'

Flo giggled.

The day Father Dila had gone looking for Ozoo with his thoughts and emotions in turmoil, the priest had seriously thought of seeking out Flo and telling her to keep off him. He didn't quite agree with Ozoo's suggestion that he should get himself at least one young woman from among those the local folks considered no longer eligible for marriage and go steady with her. No, he couldn't accept that line of thinking since that would amount to a betrayal of his vocation, a negation of the very essence of priesthood.

That night, surprisingly, he had dreamt about Flo. He and Flo in a swimming pool in Italy, splashing water into each other's faces, she, scantily dressed in a bikini and he, in a pair of brief pants. He, taking hold of Flo by the shoulders and looking deeply into her eyes and Flo opening her mouth and closing it wordlessly, as if gasping for breath, choking on what she wanted to say but couldn't get out.

Then he was tracing circles around the hard nipple of Flo's congested breast with a finger, delicately, with the other hand down in the water groping under the bikini for the matted triangle of hair, fingers finding it and massaging it, kneading that surprisingly warm mound of yielding coarseness and Flo moaning more and more abjectly, now begging, begging him to do the needful, and he getting tumescent and then just exploding. He had woken up with a start and felt a slimy wetness on the bedsheet under him. He had torn the brief pants, sodden with man-seed, off him and thrown them angrily against the wall beyond the foot of the bed, the pants bouncing wetly off the wall and settling abjectly around one leg of the bed. He had drawn on another pair of briefs, changed the offending bedsheet, sending it sprawling to join the pants, and then had gone back to bed.

When he had been in Italy, his friends had found it difficult to understand why he never slept in pyjamas except when it was extremely cold. He had not taken the trouble to tell them that he always felt suffocated wearing pyjamas to bed, felt as if he was in a sheath of cowhide which had been wrapped around him while still fresh and then allowed to dry. And when you put a bedsheet or two and a blanket on top of that, you should certainly feel like a corpse!

That night he had not been able to sleep, not until the small hours of the morning. He had picked up a *National Geographic* magazine from the box at the head of his bed and tried to read something about Yves-Jacques Cousteau and his underwater exploits but had failed to take in anything at all, eventually even being unable to distinguish one word from another, the words seeming to run into each other and warp and skip across the pages like a multitude of fleas. He had flung the magazine back in the box.

He had felt an unfamiliar hollowness in the pit of his stomach and something like the taste of copper in his mouth. He had felt sick and dejected and irritable, a dark cloud of despair slowly engulfing him like barkcloth. He had lain on his back with his arms pillowing his head, staring up at the flaking concrete ceiling and trying to think, but to no avail. He had turned onto his belly, then onto his side then again onto his back, but still could neither sort out his thoughts nor go to sleep.

He had got up and gone to the bathroom and used two full basins of very cold water for bathing and then gone back to the bedroom and desperately thrown himself onto the bed, praying 'God take this thorn out of my flesh,' but still he hadn't fallen asleep...

Until the small hours of the morning. Until the cocks began to crow and flutter and hop down from their roosts. That was when sleep had finally claimed him, coming over him in a merciful drowsiness that plunged him into oblivion without warning.

When the priest had woken up at nine, he had felt drained, exhausted and disoriented. He had stayed in bed for another hour until the old cook, worried that something bad could have happened to him, had cautiously tapped on his bedroom window and asked him was he ill and if not to open up so she could bring him his late breakfast.

* * *

'You said your husband has gone off to war?' Father Dila asked Flo.

'Yes, he's been fighting for about one and a half years now.'

'I'd thought he was an errant fisherman.'

'Fisherman he has never been, not even before the war. He was a driver then.'

'Why is it generally believed he is a fisherman?'

'A cover he created for himself. Counting on his uncle and aunt never to reveal what he actually is. And on me.'

'Now you've told me.'

'I trust you.'

'What if I told somebody else?'

'I would kill you.'

He laughed, softly, the laughter gurgling like a pebbly brook.

From whatever angle one looked at her, Flo had little physical beauty. From a narrow forehead, her head broadened towards the back so that from above it would look something like a wedge. Though very black and shiny, her hair was stiff and short and came low over her forehead, yet surprisingly steering clear of the ears and stopping abruptly at the base of the skull in a neat line.

Her arms were thick and muscular and ended in large ungainly hands that seemed more familiar with the hoe than the lighter feminine chores. Her legs, like her arms, were also thick and muscular, with short, narrow feet finishing in stubby toes. Her skin was mahogany.

Yet she was attractive. Her appearance gave one an impression of immeasurable solidity. Also, the muscular arms and legs had an intriguing suppleness to them, especially when she moved. The buttocks, broad and flat and tucked in at the lower ends, wriggled almost imperceptibly in well-coordinated rhythm with the rest of her body.

But her true beauty resided in her eyes, those large, round eyes, sometimes flecked with red, sometimes white as milk, eyes that dominated the broad flat nose with the slitted nostrils. And the mouth. There was a lot of beauty there too. While the eyes twinkled in milk-white furtive merriment, as most of the time they did now, or while they seemed to retract and become shot through with blood when Flo was sad, they always inspired affection. So did the broad, fairly thick lips, naturally purplish and sensuous, eddies of sensitivity discernible about them without being vulgarly obvious, like infinitesimal currents under a calm stream.

One surprise Flo could spring on you was her voice, low and whispery yet strong, girlish and womanly at one and the same time.

Given her build and height - she was quite tall for a woman - she would have been intimidating to most men had she not had the kind of eyes and mouth and voice she was endowed with, which betrayed a sensitivity of nature and a gentleness of disposition that were the bedrock of her character.

Perhaps it was because Flo didn't have the kind of physical beauty that exploded in your face, stunning you, that Father Dila had not taken notice of her at once, when they had initially met at the first choir practice; for then, much as he was committed to leading a life of celibacy, he recognised and appreciated feminine beauty without, of course, wanting to drag its representatives into bed with him.

'Tell me about him,' the priest said.

'About who?'

'Your husband.'

'Oh him? I told you he's a fighter, fighting the government.'

He looked sternly at her and she looked hastily away.

'What kind of man is he? What kind of husband? That's what I'd like to know.'

'You haven't met him?'

'No.'

'Well, he isn't like you, tall and slender and graceful. He's fairly short actually, shorter than me with lots of meat over his bones. He has a tendency to get fat whenever he's happy. Reminds me usually of an otter.'

'Mm. You don't seem to be very happy with him, otherwise you wouldn't be here, now would you? Say, were you forced to marry him?'

'No,' she protested forcefully, almost violently. 'I'm the kind of person who could never have been forced to marry anybody, not even the President!' And she giggled.

'Then why - why did you get married to someone who made you so sad and miserable? At least that's what I think you were before you met me!' He was teasing her, trying to find out whether her feelings for him went deep enough.

'Don't flatter yourself. Any other man could have been the same,' and she affectionately pinched his ear, then went on to knead it.

'Well, what cruel things does he do to you?' Reassured now of Flo's love for him, he felt it was safe to delve deeper. 'Does he beat you up occasionally?'

She kept silent for some time, then she spoke.

'No, his violence is not of that kind. It is a violence he keeps stored up in his heart and that comes out only when you're in bed making love.'

'Oh dear,' Father Dila gasped. He had heard about the sort of cruelties some men inflicted on their wives even while in the very act of love-making and he thought they were sordid things to do to a woman.

'What's wrong? Don't you want to hear anymore about it?' she asked.

He wanted to say no, because he felt the revelations would hurt him more deeply than the cruelties would have done the object of the violence, yet he was driven by a relentless curiosity to know as much as possible about this shadowy figure who was the husband of this woman who was still very much a girl.

'Well, since you've begun, you might as well finish.' He was resigned now to whatever possible hurt the revelations would bring.

'He will come back from drinking – he prefers *waragi* – hop into bed and then just mount you. Then he will pound away until he gets exhausted and drops off like a leach and goes straightaway to sleep. With his back turned to you. And all the time he's sleeping with you, you're aware his mind is elsewhere, not on another woman you could find out about and track down and beat up, but just far away thinking thoughts that you can't get to know about even when you ask him.'

Tears had begun to well up in Flo's large eyes.

'I can see you still love him,' said the priest. Despite his wanting her all for himself, he felt pity for this woman with the gentle, affectionate heart who had got married to a vile, brutal son-of-a-bitch who didn't even know how to make a decent job of lovemaking.

'Yes, I do. In fact even as a child I worshipped him.'

'Well, well, well.'

'The worst part of it all is that he doesn't even care to say those nice little things that make a woman happy. Or make those little complaints that make a woman feel her presence around the house is noticed by her husband, complaints that might lead to a little quarrel and sulking and then to bed and reconciliation. He neither says 'thank you,'nor does he complain. And when I complain, he just ignores it. When he's away, I really long for him, but the moment he comes back, 'I feel like I have a walking corpse under my roof.'

The tears were coming fast and thick now, in big drops that landed on the pillow and stained it, as Father Dila shifted his arm from her waist to her shoulders and drew her close to him, hugging her, trying to bring consolation to the poor girl, this poor woman with the heart bleeding from the spear-thrust of scornful ingratitude and unrequited affection.

'What drew me to him was what attracted all the other girls to him. We were all in a furious race, chasing after him, what we could see of him, what we thought he was.' She was beginning to calm down now. 'He was so self-possessed, even while still very young. And he had something in the depths of his eyes which we all wanted to find out about. Also he was very serious, always having a scornful look on his face for the girls and only talking to whichever of us he choose to talk with once, and then forgetting her completely after that. And never ever seeming to be really hungry for our company or trying to impress us. We went mad with frustration, even young as we were, especially since he would always be the brightest boy in class and, though poor, also the smartest. When he went to secondary school, he'd built up such a reputation for himself that we'd all become besotted with him, me most of all.'

'And this is the prize,' said the priest.

'Yes, this is the prize.'

'How many children d'you have?'

'One.'

'How old?'

'Four going on five.'

'Hey, you must have been married for quite some time.'

'Yes, four years now.'

'And all that time he's been treating you this way?'

'No. It all began around the time he lost his driver's job. About two years ago.'

'What a pity!'

'Yes, it's a pity, but what can I do?'

'Divorce him.'

'How? With all the cattle gone, where would my parents find the animals to refund his bridewealth? In any case, I still love him, I still love him very much. If only he could change!'

She was wringing her hands as if she wanted to destroy them. Always in her mind's eye she could see Apire. He always hovered there, obstinate, never budging, much of the time blocking out everything else so that she at times even became irritated by, impatient with her son who might frantically be seeking attention. Apire of the sad eyes. Apire with the bitter, derisive expression on his face... with the firm, immobile mouth... who didn't speak most of the time and didn't seem to be aware of what was taking place around him. Apire shiny-black and stout, almost chubby, but very intelligent and spry like a wild cat on those short legs of his. Apire at first refusing even to look at her and she hurting inside like a street child. Then one day sitting under a tree with her, talking calmly, confidently about what he intended to do in future. Then ignoring her for weeks after that. She pining for him all that time, tramping after him like an orphan, hoping for another chance for just such a chat as they had had, fearing to get too close to him lest he turn the full heat of his scorn on her, yet feeling all the time that the scorn was there just the same, stamped like a seal on that immobile face, scorn meant for her, withering her pride to the size of a shrivelled pea. Yet she pushed on, valiantly, never giving up, signalling to him from that distance she always kept: I love you, I love you, I love you...! Then long, oh so long after that, Apire asking her, Can you come to our home this afternoon? and she saying eagerly:

Yes! yes! yes! without stopping to think. Apire taking her to bed that day, without talking much, just stripping her naked and asking her to sit next to him, Apire stroking her breasts and thighs and kissing her... the tension from residual fear of him easing out of her body and she feeling herself swell for him and he pushing her gently down and she stretching out on her back on his crudely-made bed with the cotton-stuffed mattress, and he passionately mounting her... Later the episode getting known at school and the teasing from the boys and the jealousy and envy and spite of the girls pouring over her like hot syrup, and she loving Apire all the more.

'...' and then go home?' The priest's voice jerked her out of her reverie.

'What did you say?'

'I think it's time you washed and went back home. Your people might be wondering where you are.'

'They think I come to the mission for choir practice and to learn the fine needlecraft those nuns teach. They can't suspect anything. At least not yet, since this is only the first time.'

'It might be the first time, but you'd better be very careful. I don't want to end up with a bullet in my stomach, seeing that your husband is a soldier.' His tone was both serious and bantering.

'Rebel,' she corrected, adding, 'You're the one who should be careful. Sending that Caroline girl to me to tell me in everybody's hearing that the nuns wanted to see me! What if Caroline talks? Or somebody asks the nuns and they say I never was with them?'

'Caroline is my niece and I know enough about her to believe she wouldn't talk. As for the nuns, well, who would want to ask such silly questions of them and for what reason?' He knew he didn't sound very convincing but wasn't sure whether there could have been any better answer.

'Well, then, that's that,' Flo said.

'Now go wash up and go home clean,' the priest said, pinching Flo's bottom as she sat up and swivelled round to set her feet down on the floor. She got up and plodded away to the bathroom.

That night he had had the dream about Flo and himself splashing water at each other and had woken up to a bedsheet slimy with semen. Father Dila had realised that he had been in love with Flo longer than he had been mentally aware of. But it had been a vague sort of love, something faint and unassertive that had required Flo's blurted confession to emerge. He had tried to place the exact moment when he had begun to love her and had traced it to the episode when Flo had sung off-key and had asked if she could come over and stand next to him.

Some kind of empathy had established itself between them from that moment, something both physical and spiritual that did not communicate itself alone, in its own right, but submerged in the general feeling of well-being that suffused his body and soul as he stood there in front of his choir teaching them, correcting them, guiding them, immersed in them and their singing.

After Flo's confession, the sluices of all the different human emotions had given way in him, the different waters mixing, swirling about him in a great buffeting rush that had distracted him until he had talked to Ozoo and had had the dream. Then he knew he was damned. There was no question of backing off now. He was in love and he wasn't going to be caught pretending that he was the kind of man who could go on resisting the allure of women for ever and ever. Flo was a housewife, yes, but he had felt that turning her down would have been cruel self-denial, that it would have hurt him more than he had the capacity to endure.

Flo was coming back, he could hear her tripping jauntily along the corridor that ran the full length of the Mission House along a north-south axis. Soon she showed up at the bedroom door, bathed and fresh, a towel wrapped around the lower part of her body, leaving the flat belly with the almost imperceptible stretch-marks and the big, hanging breasts bare, her feet squelching noisily in the priest's sandals.

'You didn't take long.' Father Dila swallowed hard, trying to conceal the atavistic gleam of desire in his eyes. He could feel his body getting hot all over and his manhood beginning to swell.

'Oh, I took quite some time. Perhaps you didn't want me back so soon?' she teased.

'Could you please sit down here a moment,' he patted the spot next to his midriff, like a wild-cat that has spied a chicken-run. She unhooked the towel and pulled it off her, then flung it into his face, laughing, all in one deft movement.

'No, not that again,' she said, 'Time's running short and I have to leave before your catechumens begin popping in to find out what's happening with their beloved padre.'

She dressed quickly, patted him on the ribcage, skipped lightly to the door and exited, closing it with a soft click behind her. He heard her padding away along the corridor in her slippers, heard the creaking of the dining-room door as it opened and closed and knew she was gone. He got up and went to the bathroom, wondering why she should have used his sandals for bathing and not her own slippers. Was it the tendency he had noticed in his sisters to use articles of dress and other things that belonged to their lovers or husbands? Or was it simply caution? Was it perhaps because she didn't want to reach home wearing freshly-washed slippers? Well, whatever it was, that was her businness not his!..

After her initial confession of love to Father Dila, Flo had kept away from choir practice, away from Church Service, had simply plunged out of sight. At first he hadn't minded much, thinking silly girl, silly little big cow of a girl, perhaps your indiscretion has embarrassed you and you're trying to give yourself time to forget it, to allow it to blow over, before you resurface.

After she had kept resolutely away for one week, not even putting in an appearance at Sunday service, he had been gripped by a sudden bout of despair and the subsequent sessions of choir practice had begun to lose their thrill. From mealtime to prayer to choir practice to bedtime, he never stopped thinking about her, wondering had she decided she'd done a stupid thing declaring herself to him shamelessly like that? Was she therefore trying to regret the upsurge of emotion that had spilt over that day, uncontrollable, choking her, to subside and die off before they could meet again? He worried that she might have lost interest in him after all, and that had further deepened his despair so that he had become restive and highly irritable, and on two occasions had called off choir practice altogether, claiming a non-existent sickness.

Towards the end of the second week after Flo's disappearance, when he had resorted to sedatives to woo sleep, he was surviving mainly on tea and bread, and had become quite thin and listless.

The father had also taken to shamelessly passing by the place where he knew she lived, not jogging, but riding slowly on his Comrade bicycle, and each time telling himself, take a firm grip on yourself man, don't look in the direction of her place. Until one day, panicking, he had plunged blindly into the broad path leading to her home and asked the folks he found there where she was and why did she not go for choir practice anymore? They had informed him, unsuspecting, that she had gone off to her parents and would be back in about ten days' time.

Awareness of Flo's whereabouts had brought with it a slight cooling of his overheated emotions and he had begun to sleep, fitfully, without the aid of the sedatives. At the end of the third week, she had appeared just as suddenly as she had vanished and he had had a hard time keeping his mind on the Mass he was conducting. He had not been aware of her presence until the offertory, when she had walked up the aisle of the church and deposited money daintily in the collection basket and, before turning back, had looked up at him and smiled briefly.

Her sudden appearance and smile had thrown him off balance and he had been unstable during the rest of the service, almost spilling the wine onto the altar cloth as he poured it into the chalice.

She had sneaked off immediately the Mass was ended without saying so much as a word to him, leaving him wondering whether he wasn't making a fool of himself hankering after somebody who, as far as he knew, could have lost interest in him during the three weeks she had been absent. But she'd looked up at him in church, and she'd smiled that slow fluttery, captivating smile of hers, and at him! No, he wouldn't give her up just yet, not until she began showing him in no uncertain terms that she wanted nothing to do with him in the way of a more intimate relationship than that which had already been existing between them as choirmaster and choir-member.

That afternoon, however, she had promptly turned up to attend choir practice. For the first time, he had noticed that the sadness which had made her face look like a funeral mask had lifted and had been supplemented by a glow of happiness in her eyes, as well as a secretive smile that played around the corners of her mouth throughout the whole time she was singing. He believed that she was trying to communicate something to him without the use of words. For the first time, too, he had noticed, though fleetingly, the inner beauty that lay deep within her and that was reflected in her large eyes and her sensitive mouth.

At the end of the choir practice, she had come up to him and greeted him, curtseying, had told him she had urgent things to attend to at home, and given him a full ladle of her seemingly uncertain smile and then had gone off. His heart had clenched and lurched and somersaulted, and he had realised that this was one girl, one woman, he was going to stay in love with for a very, very long time.

IV

'One times one is one
Two times two is four
Three times three is nine
Four times four is sixteen
Five times five is twenty-five....

All the teacher had to do was start Erabu and his classmates off and they would go squealing the multiplications until they reached the 'twelve times twelve is one hundred forty-four' ending.

They chanted without taking much thought for, after having practised the multiplications for days now, they had ended up learning them off by heart. Erabu didn't much care what the 'one times one is one' led to, and often wondered what connection it had with his life, but he enjoyed the chant, which always reminded him of the time lightning had struck their home, sending his sister sprawling unconscious.

The sister had run home from school on seeing clouds slowly gathering into dark, puffy masses, threatening rain. Earlier in the day, their mother had spread some sorghum and millet out in the courtyard to dry and had gone off to look for firewood. She knew their mother wouldn't be back yet.

She had arrived home and begun hand-pushing the millet from the edges of the spread into a mound in the centre. The rain had been kind, it had held off for some time. Then a drizzle had started as she began to scoop up loads of the millet in the large wicker winnowing tray and take it to their big corrugated iron-roofed house. She hadn't felt threatened, for it was a slow, uncertain drizzle that didn't seem likely to turn into a deluge.

Then the lightning had struck. It had struck the big *mabati* house, splitting the door facing the nearby murram road right down the middle. She had been flung down by the force of the crackling explosion - laid out unconscious, with her tongue turned upward and inward, blocking her throat.

People had rushed to the scene of the accident and one wise old woman had straightened out his sister's tongue. If that hadn't been done, she would have choked to death. The local Italian Catholic priest – kind old man that he was – had offered to drive her in his old pick-up to the nearest hospital situated twenty miles away.

It had been said that the rain-cock – for lightning was a huge, burnished cock with a powerful kick and it lived in anthills in the wild – it was said that this cock had entered the *mabati* house through the ruined door, the split in the timber being the spot where it had smashed its way in with its sturdy legs.

On coming out through the door facing the inner courtyard where Erabu's sister was – it had not been necessary for the rain-cock to kick this time since that door had been wide open – it had spotted her and caught her a glancing blow with the tip of its wing and then had sped off to hide in a nearby swamp before proceeding to take up residence again in its favourite anthill. All this within a matter of seconds, such was the speed with which the rain-cock went about its business.

The wise old men of the clan had gathered and planted tall stakes around the stricken homestead, cordoning it off. Then they had strung out small balls of bitter-gourd *keno* on their own vines atop the stakes. It was the presence of *keno* that would discourage the rain-cock from making further runs on a homestead it had already struck once.

Then the day had come for the balls and vines of *keno* to be taken down and carried to the swamp for which the rain-cock had headed after doing its evil deed. It was the elders who had carried the coils of vine and globes of *keno* together with two white hens which would be offered in propitiation to the spirits of the ancestors who might have sent the rain-cock. They had gone to the swamp chanting all the way, not being permitted to so much as glance behind them. They had reached the swamp, and here incantations had been made, a few mysterious rituals performed, including killing the hens by breaking their necks and disembowelling them without plucking a single feather from them. They had headed back home, in single file as before, the elders in the lead chanting incantations and the rest of them responding in unvaried refrains. They had left the hens behind, and had not been allowed to look back.

So this 'one times one is one' business always reminded him of those incantations, though he failed to figure out how a number multiplied by itself should be itself. He had for some time wanted to ask Teacher, but he didn't want to sound stupid. Teacher seemed to be so intelligent and wise that whatever he told them must surely be correct and true though he, Erabu, would have loved to believe that one times one was two.

'You're performing wonderfully, my children. Could we go over the multiplications again?'

They launched into a repeat of the multiplications with as much enthusiasm as before, for Teacher's lessons were always enjoyable. Moreover, Teacher always called them "my children" and only pinched their ears when they went wrong, unlike their parents who often laid about them with a switch of bamboo or, even worse, that of the dreaded *opobo*, lithe and stinging like a strip of sun-cured hippo-hide.

'Three times three is nine
Four times four is sixteen...'

Teacher wore beautiful clothes too, and was always clean, and never smelt of tobacco like their folks back home. When teacher spoke to you, his breath smelt nice, as if he had chewed something sweet and scented, such as bubble gum which Erabu was simply crazy about.

'Seven times seven is forty-nine
Eight times eight is sixty-four...'

Teacher had taught them two beautiful songs which he said he had learnt in a neighbouring district where he had done his teacher training course. One of them was:

Nyalo doo, nyalo doo
Kur itura kora
Inyalo doo;

Nyalo doo, nyalo doo
Kur itura kora
Injalo doo;

Rup rup rup rup
Kur itura kora
Inyalo doo

Rip rip rip rip
Kur itura kora
Inyalo dool!*

Teacher had even taken the trouble to translate this song into the local language so they could understand what they were singing. And when he sang it with them out on the football pitch, he always clapped and danced with them, bobbing up and down, tall and slender and happy. Their own fathers never did this, though Teacher was older than some of them.

'Eswilu, could you please stand up and say the multiplications alone?' Teacher was saying, 'loud enough for all your classmates to hear? Starting from six times six?'

Teacher had taught them another song which Erabu simply adored. It was a song they asked Teacher to sing with them every now and then, a song which said some mysterious thing about husbands and wives:

Joni obalo nyinga tutwal
Joni obalo nyinga tutwal
Kadi kona awoto ngwedo dek
Okobo ni awoto moyo coo!

Ani doo
Kubalo nyinga
Ai doo
Obalo nyinga
Kadi kono

* English version of song found in glossary at end of book.

Awoto moyo dek
Kukobo ni
Awoto yenyo coo!

Teacher had kindly rendered the song beautifully in the whit
man's tongue so that now they were able to sing it in English as
well!

Husband spoil my name
Husband spoil my name
Even if I go for food
He say that
I go for men.

Oh yeah!
Spoil my name
Oh yes!
Spoil my name
Even if I go for food
They say that
I go for men!

He loved school at that age, for it meant beautiful songs and
dancing in the football field and playing, especially during P.E.
when you were divided into two teams and made to compete with
each other. The teams were made to line up at opposite ends of the
field and you were given a short stick and the teacher clapped his
hands and said "go" and you sped off, running diagonally across the
football pitch and crossing your opponent's path. Running swiftly,
desperately scooting past the shiny backs of the opposing team and
speeding back towards your own team, not diagonally this time but
straight ahead, to arrive panting a few moments later at the exact spot
you had departed from. Gasping and stumbling, spent, frantically
thrusting the stick into the hand of the boy or girl standing at the
spot next to yours. Exhausted but happy as your mates hopped
up and down excitedly and patted you on the back and said "well

done". Then you went home at around one to a meal of curdled milk and cold *atap*.

Later, as he went up through Primary Four, Five and Six to reach Primary Seven – proudly called Top Class by its members – he realised that being in school wasn't all fun after all. The teachers toughened up on you and expected you to perform satisfactorily. They began to threaten you with failure at the end of the primary school course and frequently took a *kiboko* to you, giving you the kind of hiding that had your buttocks smarting the whole day.

They now frequently talked in terms of strokes of the cane and made you feel as if failing the Primary Leaving Examination was a disease worse than leprosy and TB combined and that if you ever had the misfortune to fail such an exam, then you should go to the nearest swamp and drown yourself.

Yet he didn't find things easy as a member of the much-vaunted Top Class, he didn't find things easy at all. Especially when the teacher of English began talking about irregular verbs and 'ifs' 1, 2 and 3, which many of his classmates thought were easy. He had always thought there was only one 'if'! Then the Christian Religious Education teacher would come in and begin blabbering about something called three-persons-in-one: the Father, the Son, and the Holy Spirit! Later that ugly science teacher with the eyes and nose like those of a buffalo would turn up and talk about capturing some kind of air called 'oxygen' in a glass cup or something like that; or worse still, ask them to pluck leaves from the mango trees in the school compound and try to explain to them that what made the leaves green was something called 'chloro', he couldn't even get the name right, it sounded so much like chloroquine. The teacher he hated most was the one who taught him maths because he made it sound so simple! He had a way of making you feel like an idiot if you couldn't understand what he taught. He talked about simultaneous equations and algebra and geometry the way you would talk about the difference between one goat and another. Some people were surely lucky to have been blessed with such brains!

Each day, the moment classes came to an end, Erabu would be the first to leave the classroom and go off to indulge one of his passions: football. Though he wasn't very good at the game, he played football until he was exhausted and then went home. He always made a point of returning the ball to the Games Store himself lest it should be stolen by one of the other boys. You could never trust anybody these days! If that one ball had got lost, that would have spelt disaster for Erabu.

At the end of the year, Erabu sat the Primary Leaving Examination and almost failed to make Division Three. Still his father, who loved education, succeeded in securing him a place in a rural government school – one of the so-called 'Third World Schools' – but no amount of persuasion could make Erabu join it. Then the father tried threats, but to no avail. Next he suggested Erabu should enrol in a technical school and learn at least carpentry or bricklaying or tailoring, but Erabu adamantly refused. He told his father bluntly that he was fed up with school and all he wanted to do was become a farmer and get married. After all, what was his father going to do with the more than eight hundred head of cattle he had if not allow him to take as many wives as he wanted and at the earliest possible opportunity.

Giving in at last, Erabu's father had begged him to at least agree to stay single until he was old enough to be a responsible husband and father. Erabu had agreed.

Erabu had been aware from early childhood that his father loved him deeply and would refuse him nothing since he was the only son in the family and the second-last born. Of the eight children born to Mr Malinga and Josefina - those were the names of Erabu's parents - the first six were now all married, including the twins who had come immediately before Erabu. Their marriage partly accounted for the great animal wealth Malinga had. The last born was a girl whose conception had surprised both Malinga and Josefina, for she had come at a moment when they had begun to think Josefina had already passed the age at which a woman would normally be expected to have children, six years after Erabu had been born.

Josefina loved the last born very much but simply worshipped the ground on which Erabu walked, for God had offered him to them at a time when they had already begun to despair of ever having a boy child. The birth of the twin sisters was generally attributed to Malinga's having elephantiasis of the scrotum.

Whereas at school Erabu had adored soccer, at home his first love was cattle. Somehow his love for cattle had become tied in with his love for the land.

An incomparable thrill always went coursing through his body as he ploughed the fields behind a team of straining oxen, pushing down on the handles of the plough to turn the rich, loamy soil. He loved the rank odour of the steaming animals as much as the must tang of fresh-turned earth, which never failed to tickle his nostrils. He felt good as the clods of friable soil yielded crumbling under his soles when he trod firmly on them. It soothed him to stand on the edge of a field newly planted with groundnuts and watch as big teardrops of rain peppered the field. It didn't bother him at all that he got sodden to the skin in the process, or that he might catch a cold, for the sight of the lumps of soil slowly dissolving into a rich fructifying darkness stirred in him an exhilaration that nothing else did.

It thrilled him even more when the groundnuts came up, at first a cluster of yellow-green leaves, wrinkled, delicate and tender, nestled between white halves of the original seed. Then the bits of seed would wither and drop off a few weeks later and the leaves, toughened now, would reach proudly, fearlessly upwards, dark green and shiny like oilcloth.

He loved the harvest. The pulling up of the mature plants with their nuts now hardened and ribbed and fibrous. The tearing away of the nuts from the bases of the plants to which they still clung, tenacious and yielding only to a hard pull. At the end of the day, some of the groundnuts would be roasted under a heap of burning grass. Then the family would assemble around the mound of groundnuts gleaned from among the black ashes and bits of unburnt grass, cracking the nuts open with their fingers to reach the pink or red heat-shrivelled seeds within. You plucked out the seeds and popped them into your mouth, and as you chewed, they crunched beautifully, giving off a buttery fragrance.

Even as he thought of the land and its fecundity, at the back of Erabu's mind were always the cattle. The land could only be conceived of in terms of the cattle. Life was possible only because of the existence of cattle.

When a bull or a cow became too old to be useful, you killed it and smoked most of the meat and stored it in the granary. You stretched the skin out in the sun to dry and you used it later to sleep on.

When a calf died at birth you didn't throw it away, for that would bring ill luck: all the calves that would be born thereafter would also die. You instead skinned the dead calf and cut it up and smoked it, and later your father ate it with his male friends and the youngest children, for neither mature women nor young men and women were permitted by custom to touch such meat. It was a taboo you grew up with, a taboo you didn't question.

When you were hungry, you milked a cow and drank the milk fresh and creamy and warm with a mound of *atap*. Or you looked for curdled milk or skimmed milk where Mother had carefully stored it away and you drank it straight from the big calabash.

You gave the animals you loved names like Lomongin and Opio and Nyerere, except the dogs of course, which you often named Amin or Hitler or Dayan or Stalin because of their fierceness. You put out your hand for the cattle to lick with their rough, slobbering tongues. It was a joy to watch the calves, frightened or simply excited, suddenly swing back their ears and caper stiffly away with their tails up in the air.

Sometimes you rode on the back of a friendly bullock, moving among the other cattle like a king while they munched on the tender grass, healthy and contented and nonchalant. Or you induced two big bulls from rival kraals to fight around the clayey anthill where the cattle daily congregated to bite away chunks of the salty soil before going off to the nearby dam for water. The bulls often fought violently, locking horns and pushing each other skidding amidst clusters of flying turf and swirling clouds of dust. The long, heavy testicles of the animals swung and swayed like clubs and their big humps bunched up with vitality even as they leaned sideways on the powerful shoulders. As the animals disengaged and pawed and huffed and snuffed and bellowed manfully and glowered at each other before locking horns once again you supported the bull from your father's kraal, calling him by all the fancy names you could think of. Then when one of the bulls, admitting defeat, suddenly turned tail and fled, you herded your animals to the watering point. At the end of the fight you could almost hear the sigh of the cows, who would have been following the tussle with a lot of interest and wide-eyed excitement, a sigh of disappointment that it should all have ended so soon.

On the days you took the animals out to graze, you returned home at dusk, tired, grimy and sticky with sweat, sometimes wet from the rain, but always happy. You returned home to find a big calabash of *adere* waiting for you. You poured boiling water into the pale-yellow beer and it swirled and fizzed almost inaudibly, and a rash of frothy bubbles sallied forth from deep within it, bursting silently on the surface. You clamped your lips to the rim of the calabash and sucked in the warm bitter-sweet liquid, sieving out the dregs which at times clung to your lips. You could not help sighing with contentment after each draught of the invigorating beverage. Life was good!

* * *

'Encore! Encore!'

The two-speaker super-bass radio cassette was silent for some time as the popular South African number was rewound. Suddenly there was a loud thump. The record had struck up again.

They were all young, this crowd. Youth parties were a must on important occasions such as Easter and Independence anniversaries and at Christmas as well as on New Year's Day. Every youth made it a point of honour to contribute in cash and kind towards the organisation of such parties, or take an active part in their organisation, in order to earn the right to be present at them. If you avoided such gatherings, some of which involved up to two hundred youths, you were dubbed 'anti-social'.

A week before this particular Christmas, one of the young men at the party had purchased a Hitachi radio-cassette with the proceeds from the cow ghee and dried slices of cassava that he had taken to the City for sale.

To the frenzied drumming and soulful singing blaring from the new radio, the young bodies dipped and gyrated in a ferment of syncopated rhythm. Nobody could have been happier than Erabu on this day as he too bobbed up and down and swung round among the throng of young people, Esina in front of him, Esina dancing enraptured and sensuous and ecstatic, her rapt eyes staring up past his shoulder at the star-spangled vault of the sky. He was the happiest man on earth as he grabbed Esina around the waist and gyrated with her, her long white-and-blue print skirt billowing behind her ample posterior like a cylindrical flag, as he sprang nimbly away from her and spun on one leg, then reached out for her again and hugged her tight, both of them swinging to left and right, to and fro, in an exhilarating intimacy of perfectly synchronised movement.

'Oh dear, the speed with which you dance! It would require one with the nimbleness of a mountain goat to keep up,' Esina remarked, giggling breathlessly.

'And you're that mountain goat, my duiker,' said Erabu, laughing.

'Don't call me that again, you rascal,' and she thumped his back.

'Call you what, duiker?'

They both burst out laughing. He knew that despite her vehement remonstrances, she liked the name.

He had first noticed the similarity between Esina and the duiker when he had been watching one that had been captured while still a doe and reared by a neighbour like an orphan child. From the near-almond eyes, with the large deep-black pupils that looked almost purple, to the heart-shaped head with the high cheekbones, to the thin nose with the slightly uptilted tip and the small full-lipped mouth that was always in a pout, she looked like a duiker. She appeared to resemble a duiker even more from the long, slender neck and the deep, narrow chest with the small breasts, down to the slender waist and the slightly flaring hips that tapered off to legs which were long and shapely and supple. Her feet were long and beautifully arched, and had long tapering toes with toenails that had a nacreous sheen to them. Yet incongruously, she possessed a well-endowed rear that excited a lot of jealousy and envy among the womenfolk. She gave you the impression of being light and nimble and energetic even while seated.

You felt Esina was tall until you got close to her, and then you realised with shock that she was actually quite short. At sixteen, she already looked very mature and ripe and ready for childbearing.

'What are you thinking about?' she asked Erabu.

'Why do you think I am thinking about something?'

'You aren't dancing as vigorously as you were doing a few moments ago. In fact, you're even dancing out of step.'

'Oh that!' Erabu paused a bit. 'I was thinking about us.'

'What about us?'

'About why you should be here dancing with me, with my arm around your waist. About why you should be so much in love with me - or seem to be so much in love - when there are so many handsome young men around. Young men who would give everything they have for a chance to marry you and keep you forever!'

'What do you think those boys have that you don't have?'

'I've neither beauty of body nor intelligence, yet this place is simply *crawling* with boys who're handsome and are in secondary school. Young people whose parents possess a lot of animals too.'

'Oh dear, what stupid thoughts to have on such a day as this!'

'You know I've always wondered what could have attracted you to me in the first place!'

'Perhaps I just found myself loving you more than I could tell.'

If there was one thing Erabu had no illusions about, it was his looks. He was tall, big-boned and meaty, but in a rather awkward-looking, loose-limbed way. His hands were large and thick and rough from work, and the fingers thick like yellow-bananas. To make it worse, he had often mused unhappily, the fingernails were arched like the back of a tortoise, and they were thick and a dirty-brown, with black stripes running parallel up over the curve and down to their tips. His feet fared no better either, for they were flat and splayed and the toenails looked exactly like the fingernails. His hair was scattered over his head in small tight knots that resembled goats' droppings turned black, and the bare spaces between them had the unhealthy appearance of something sprinkled with wood ash.

His eyes were protruberant and vulnerable-looking and the arched bridge of his nose abruptly dropped to a ball-like tip with tiny holes for nostrils. His mouth was an uncharacteristically thin-lipped gash across the face.

'I'm tired, can we go and sit down?' Esina said, firmly guiding him to their seat, two of tens of other seats set in a circle around a big pot bristling with sucking tubes like porcupine quills. Once they were both seated, she emitted a short, furtive laugh. That was another thing about her that Erabu found irresistible: she laughed as if she didn't want to be caught at it!

'What's funny?' asked Erabu.

'What you've been thinking about. I mean what you said about those secondary school boys.'

Esina's voice always made Erabu want to enfold her in his arms and never let her go. That voice that was deep and husky, that rasped and cooed at one and the same moment, and always managed to drip with warmth and affection. "Have they gone and done something to you now?" He was getting jealous, he could feel the beginnings of jealousy stirring slowly within him like a waking python.

'One of them likes to visit our home. Always comes wearing the school badge, under the pretext of helping my younger brother with his schoolwork. But I know that all the time he's teaching my brother, he's all eyes for me, judging from the way his voice carries across the courtyard from my brother's hut. And he always insists on speaking English, shouting at the top of his voice, trying to impress.'

She laughed again. Erabu was now firmly gripped in the coils of his jealousy, hot and suspicious and gulping truculently.

'Which boy is that so that I teach him a little lesson now?'

'I won't tell you because I don't want you to start a fight here." Her voice was calm, soothing. She was used to the explosions of temper of this human buffalo of a boyfriend of hers. 'Tomorrow I'll give you the letter he wrote to me. It's written entirely in English, long words that I never met in school. I wonder whether you'll understand them.'

'Give me that letter and I'll know what I'll do with it. It'll end up where it belongs, deep inside a latrine pit.'

'No, you won't do any such thing. You will keep the letter so that when you marry me, it will always serve to remind you of how much I loved you.'

Erabu sulked.

One thing that Erabu didn't know about himself was that he had lots of charm. The moments when he threw a tantrum, as he was doing now, were few and far between. He didn't have much imagination, granted, and he thought and talked ponderously, but most of the time he exuded an inner warmth, an exuberance that was infectious. He was unfailingly polite and always ready to help whenever help was need. He looked out on the world with eyes that were dull but never bitter, their sharp protruberance often softened by the kindness discernible in their depths. Occasionally, Erabu waxed humorous, too.

V

Christus vincit
Christus regnat
Christus, Christus imperat

Father Santo Dila sang without enthusiasm. His usual ardour had become diluted at first, then had simply evaporated. He was beginning to find this two-week retreat more and more meaningless, nay, more irritating even.

Johannes summo pontifici...

Hypocrisy! He had never thought he would be a hypocrite like these others, these fellow retreatants standing in mock supplication to a God whose existence few of them believed in...

Et universali patri...

Apostates, but worse, much worse than those lawyers and policemen who took bribes or teachers who slept with their students.

Fax vita
Et salus perpetua...

Here they all were, bleating emptily in homage to a Pope they principally conceived of as the guarantor of their material comfort, his role as their spiritual shepherd hovering precariously on the periphery of their thoughts.

Francisco reverendissimo episcopo...

That bishop whom most of them thought was always throwing a spanner in the works. What right had he to stop them having wives stashed away in remote villages, or contracting secret marriages, when he himself had a harem of bickering concubines in the Nurses' Quarters and the convent?

Et in terra el commisso...

Certainly it was much, much better leading a straight-forward life of sin than indulging in sin behind a curtain of immaculate cassock.

Pax vita

Et salus perpetua

I believe if we turn up at Hell' gate tomorrow – if there's a hell – it's going to be "get those priests, get those damned priests, hurl them into the fire" amidst kicks and *ngwara* and slaps and scratches from all those foul-smelling demons.

Tempera bona veniant...

Let's hope so, let's hope good times will come here and in the hereafter.

Pax Christi veniat...

No peace, no peace at all! Not with all these conflicting emotions torturing me like a swarm of bluebottles.

Regnum Christi veniat.

When that promised kingdom comes, maybe things will change. Perhaps then we shall become genuinely suffused with this faith which most other times we only pay lip-service to.

Christus vincit

CIristus regnat

CIristus, Christus imperat.

Father Dila had stopped singing long before the song came to an end. He was too far gone in his irreverent thoughts to care much about the singing anyway, though from force of habit, he allowed it to keep humming in his head.

Double standards. He hated them, and he had made frantic attempts at steering clear of them. Now here he was, faced with a serious dilemma, something that struck at the very core, the essence, of his calling. He had always despised hypocrites and had desperately hoped and prayed that he would not end up being one. One time he had almost been made to feel he was one when he was bluntly asked whether he believed in 'that trash' – yes, his challenger had called it 'trash' – about the poor being blessed and the automatic inheritors of the kingdom of heaven. If so, the man had added, why did he own a Suzuki car and live in 'sumptuous' surroundings? It had required a bit of convoluted reasoning to try to convince the man that the Bible talked about 'the poor in spirit' and not the poor in the sense of 'materially deprived'. But the questioner, not to be put off, had come back with: 'Now what would poor in spirit mean?' This had led to further mental juggling until the priest had become hopelessly entangled in the finespun spider web of his own reasoning. His questioner had emitted a cold, harsh laugh and had reminded him of the glowing terms in which the Bible spoke of poor Lazarus and had haughtily marched away, leaving him in no doubt at all that his arguments had not been convincing in the least!

He had been in a glowering mood for two days after that, not even the choir practice on the first day being able to lift his spirits. He had walked about with hunched shoulders, sombrely wondering whether in taking up the priesthood he had not embarked on a life of deliberate falsehood, whether he wasn't living a sordid lie, performing empty rituals so that he could have a loaf of bread on his table and a warm blanket over his sated belly at the end of the day.

There was hypocrisy and double standards everywhere one turned.

Now look at those lawyers who sentenced somebody to a term of imprisonment for stealing a banana, one single *bogoya*, when that person was in fact in desperate need of food, and then went off in the evening to receive a bribe of half a million shillings from the relatives of a murder suspect.

Or the policemen who arrested poor housewives residing in a slum for brewing *waragi* in order to raise school fees for their children, while their own wives were engaged in exactly the same kind of activity in the barracks under the very nose of the local police chief.

Hypocrisy as embodied by some teachers who went around asserting that theirs was a 'noble profession' when they didn't have a single cent in their pockets. He personally didn't see much nobility in thickly patched trouser-seats covering thin backsides, or incapacity to feed, decently clothe, and educate one's children. Emphatic verbal denial of the usefulness of money when you didn't have it wouldn't make you any more noble than those beggars slouching around the city like grounded marabou stork. He believed that it was all a matter of somebody belatedly discovering that the coveted but inaccessible grape was sour after all. He would have dearly loved to have had an opportunity to hurl a fat wad of banknotes amidst those teachers even as they mouthed that suspect "noble profession" and seen whether their Impoverished Nobilities didn't fight to get their hungry fingers on the money.

Or the *Mulokole* who bellowed 'Praise God!' while pinching the backside of the voluptuous girl seated next to him.

And here he himself was, with arms folded like a praying mantis, giving the Monsignor at the altar the impression that he was immersed up to his scalp in prayer while all he was doing was giving free reign to blasphemous thoughts, and all this right within the holy precincts of the chapel of St. Peter's Seminary! He wondered why nobody had yet seen fit to burn him at the stake!

'Mass is ended, and may God's blessing go with you,' intoned the Monsignor, startling Father Dila out of his reverie. 'In the name of the Father, the Son and the Holy Spirit.'

Father Dila shambled silently out of the chapel. Stealthily glancing at the sanctimonious yet strangely closed faces around him, wondering whether the same kind of thoughts had been passing through their minds.

He retired straightaway to the room allocated to him for the duration of the retreat and promptly began to think of Flo. Thinking about Flo reminded him about the article he had had published in the *Osservatore Nuovo* while still in Italy. He had kept the newspaper in sound condition in a folder and stored it in the mahogany bookcase in the Mission. He had brought it with him to the retreat along with other newspapers and magazines and books. Now he set about reading the article for the third time in two weeks.

'One basic weakness of Christianity,' the article ran, including Catholicism, is that it has abjectly failed to be conceived of as something that should be an integral part of their lifestyles by the majority of its practitioners, among whom the faith was forcibly introduced from outside, instead of being allowed to be inducted into their cultures as a result of the inner dynamic, the natural evolution, of those respective cultures themselves. Such induction would doubtless have led to an automatic and effortless interiorisation of the principles and values of Christianity by the peoples among whom it spread, thus moulding their thought processes and their conduct, their modes of dress, as well as their attitude towards important social and political issues. Unfortunately, however, Christianity is often perceived as an alien set of beliefs that one is taught while being prepared for baptism or confirmation or matrimony, beliefs that urge a certain set of responses that are not always consonant with, and at times are set in direct opposition to, those practices and morals that have over the years become deeply ingrained in the fabric of a people's political and social life. So for the majority of such peoples, Christianity remains an alien faith - even an alienating faith for its more devout adherents - something that one dons when it is expedient to do so, only to be cast off when there is no longer any need for the people for whose attention it had been put on to continue being impressed.

'The liturgies of the various Christian denominations are strange and were for sometime in the past, especially in the Catholic Church, conducted in tongues the native peoples did not comprehend. The clergy are often viewed as standard-bearers of a conquering faith that often enriches them, but that makes them lost to their traditional cultures.

'I should like to concentrate mainly on Catholicism, its liturgy and its clergy in my own country in Africa, for that is what I know best about.

'Catholicism is not considered to have the capacity to take on an African complexion because it has its nerve-centre here in Rome and its far-flung outposts derive, or are generally believed to derive, their life-blood and sustenance from Rome. That is exactly what the ramifications of the Catholic church are perceived as: outposts of a European, at times even Italian, faith, this impression being strengthened by the presence of a large contingent of white, especially European, missionaries in Africa – the Verona congregation, the Mill Hill Fathers, the White Fathers, the Holy Cross Missionaries, etc. The African clergy, who however constitute the majority, are viewed as hovering on the periphery of the clerical establishment, marginalised, powerless, belonging neither with the white clergy nor with the black laity.

'Almost everything about the Catholic Church is white. Grape wine is not indigenous to Africa, nor is the wheat from which the Host is made. The tabernacles and altars are modelled upon those found in Europe, and they are often manufactured on that continent and then freighted to Africa in pieces that only need to be assembled. The vestments are of Europe, and so are the bishop's sceptre and mitre. Many of the church buildings are either Romanesque or Gothic and thus look like small-scale models of cathedrals and chapels in Europe. The only concession that has been made to African indigenous cultures lies in the realms of language and song, for the African congregations can now use their diverse languages to say prayers they can understand and to sing songs set to tunes they enjoy, and to the accompaniment of musical instruments they themselves have created.

'The African clergy have failed to find a firm footing among the people in the midst of whom they live and work, for they are often treated like aliens, not quite belonging with the people living around the Mission House. They are an elite who drive cars and ride motorcycles. They eat the white man's food and live in houses built by him. They often drink the white man's beverages and listen to his music: classical music by Chopin and Bach and Schumann

and Beethoven and Mozart. Above all, they do not marry. That
alone sets them apart as a species of mankind who are devotees of
a God that makes very severe demands on his acolytes. Granted,
the Catholic Church has a strong following in most parishes, and
a remarkable amount of respect is shown to the priests by the laity,
but much of this respect, I suspect, owes its existence to the awe
inspired by a sound formal education and possession of property that
the ordinary Christian cannot dream of ever owning. Celibacy and
bachelorhood for clergy are therefore viewed as a necessary sacrifice
on the altar of those material possessions which are coveted by the
majority of poor laity but which happen to be inaccessible to them.
Bachelorhood should therefore, in the eyes of the laity, be only a
temporary condition one should suffer with a view to acquiring the
coveted possessions.

"In view of the foregoing, ways and means should be contemplated
of bringing Catholicism, and Christianity generally, within the
cultural ambit of the peoples of Africa, so that they can accept
and assimilate the faith with greater ease. This will ensure that the
end product is a true convert so suffused with Christianity that his
every thought, his every utterance, his every deed, is an indubitable
reflection of Christian principles and values. Perhaps the Moslems
have something to teach us in this respect in the way the majority
of them are so completely immersed in the teachings of the Koran,
in the values and practices of Islam, that it is virtually impossible to
convert them to other faiths."

Father Dila laughed, an uncharacteristically barking, hollow laugh
that was full of scorn for himself and mockery for his determination
at the time he wrote that article to strive to be the perfect priest, living
out the cardinal Christian principles, never betraying any important
tenet of Catholic doctrine, never breaking the vow of chastity even
under the stiffest of pressures.

Yet here he was, obsessed with Flo, feeling like a hound that had
tasted fresh blood and hungering for more, and right in the midst
of retreat! He wondered whether anything could break the curse put
on man on the day of his banishment from Eden.

VI

After the murder of his father and brother by state security agents, Apire had looked on with alarm as his mother had gone slowly but inexorably to pieces. He had noticed his sister, Betty, seventeen now, take on the responsibilities of foster motherhood, initially selling off all the household property that they didn't need to raise money for their school fees and clothing and whatever food they didn't grow on the sizeable plot of land behind their house. Betty had become a particularly firm taskmistress, keeping them at whatever job she wanted done, either around the house or behind it on their patch of land, with an unwavering determination that both scared and fascinated her brothers, Apire and Acaye.

Betty was generous with her mother, always giving her the money she needed whenever she went broke. She had become very enterprising, brewing *waragi* or *kwete* or *malwa* in the evenings when she returned from school and asking her mother to sell it in her absence. Whenever she could spare a little time from her school routine, Betty would rush off to the nearby villages to buy perishable foodstuffs - especially oranges and tomatoes and cabbages - which she later sold in front of their house.

But their mother had become a disappointing wreck, at times drinking much of the *waragi* – she never touched *malwa* or *kwete* claiming they disturbed her stomach – that Betty left her to sell. In retaliation, Betty would decide to lock the liquor away in the pantry and sell it herself in the evenings and on weekends. Then the mother would fret and whine and implore her for only one little tot.

She would give her the one 'little' tot, but her mother would ask for 'just one more'... then another... and yet another, until she became dead drunk. Betty would withhold the *waragi* at first, but eventually give in, tearfully, for though she didn't want her mother to drink so much, she understood the origin of her mother's craving for alcohol. Furthermore, she knew that if she didn't give her the booze she needed, she would go off and get it elsewhere anyway. Possibly from men, who would exact a price, which price her mother had of late become inclined to pay unquestioningly.

Apire loved and respected Betty, though he at times resented her authority, her no-nonsense attitude towards them. He knew, even young as he was, that it was because of them – his mother, Acaye, and himself – that Betty had left the boarding secondary school where she had been a student when their father had been killed, and had sought a place in a day school near their home. Nobody had been ready to help them, for his father had been an only child.

To show that he appreciated what Betty was doing for them, Apire tried very hard to be diligent both at home and in school, and succeeded much of the time. He also swore to himself never to insult her, though she caned him sometimes, and was always prepared to defend her when other boys said unkind things about her or abused her. On one or two occasions, he had picked a fight in her defence, once even taking on a boy called Lama who was older than him, breaking his head with a stone.

The boy's mother, fat and flabby, her breasts sagging down her front like a pair of giant pawpaws, had come puffing to their home to complain to their mother, dragging Lama behind her like a goat on a leash. The spot on his head where the stone had made contact was an ugly scarlet mush. His mother, who had always seemed to him listless and languorous with booze or hangover, had shown a surprising alacrity and presence of mind that day, spitting and hitting back like a cornered cat.

On reaching the forecourt, and finding Maria seated in a none-too-clean *gomesi* on the verandah, emptily staring into space, Lama's mother, Karamella, had halted in front of her. Then, with arms akimbo and breasts heaving and falling with anger, she had bellowed in a voice that would have made even the most strident drill sergeant sound like a eunuch.

'You fail to control your naughty children and they go scattering all over the place breaking the heads of other people's children, and then you just gape at me like a dead fish. Stupid woman, today I'll show you that I'm a true daughter of Oyengo!'

His mother hadn't at first reacted in any decisive way, only giving a little weary, unconcerned smile, which had further stoked the fat woman's anger.

'Your brat almost murders my little boy and you simply sit there grinning like a stretching cat. I have a mind to give you a proper hiding, you and that son of yours who never seems to have enough soap in the house to wash himself with!'

Maria, still grinning sheepishly, had come unstuck from the glazed cement of the verandah, unwinding slowly like a narrow bedsheet and standing up erect and proud at last, proud like a Songhai princess, though her face had taken on a highly noticeable puffiness and she had developed pouches under her eyes from heavy drinking.

'Listen Karamella,' she had said calmly, 'I have only three living children, and Betty is too old to scamper around like a piglet. Now who are these children who go *scattering* all over the neighbourhood killing other people's children?'

'Just look at my child's head!' Karamella was aflame now. Yes come right here and look at his broken head then go ahead and laugh at it because that is what your brat wanted you to do!'

Karamella was stationary, exactly the way a big granary would be stationary, the only movement about her being the rise and fall of her papaya breasts in between fat-greased bawling.

'Let me tell you one thing, Karamella,' Maria said at last, "if there's one thing that's notorious for spewing things that scatter, it's that cotton-bale stomach of yours.' Karamella gulped down a huge volume of air, giving Maria time to add: 'No wonder the floor of the communal latrine is always plastered with running shit!'

Betty and Apire, who had been listening intently with backs pressed against the end-wall of the house, ran round to the back, whooping with laughter.

Karamella piped up, 'You foul-smelling snatcher of other people's husbands, always hawking your thing cheap like a piece of bad meat.'

Maria's answer came back pat: 'I guess the men find my thing more interesting than that bog between your squelching thighs.'

Karamella winced visibly, reeling inwardly. But still she didn't move. Her son was craning his neck from behind her as if from the shelter of a giant barrel.

'You're a shame to women,' Karamella said, her composure regained, 'a drunkard, a slut and a whore.' Maria didn't interrupt her as Karamella gulped down another intake of air. 'I think somebody should get a battalion of randy men to be camped in your house so that you stop casting your sex-maddened eyes on our husbands.'

'I'm a widow, Karamella,' Maria was cold as glass. 'But for the entire time my husband was alive, I happen to have found him very satisfying, unlike some fat and flabby women whose children do not resemble their husbands.'

Karamella was stung, Maria knew, for she saw her wince again, but she didn't take so much as a step towards Maria. They stared at each other silently for some time, neither winking nor moving.

Maria now knew for certain that despite her sweaty bulk, Karamella was a coward. She was one of those women who believed their vast physical dimensions would turn the knees of whoever they chose to challenge to water with fright. Though at the beginning she had been quite frightened of this bawling hippo of a woman, now her fear had vanished and she was actually spoiling for a fight.

'Any decent woman,' Karamella said finally, 'would have been expected to support her children, instead of encouraging her teenage daughter to peddle herself to feed both her and her unruly kids.'

Maria knew Betty was a far cry from this picture of her Karamella was painting for her consumption.

'I know of at least one woman,' retorted Maria, 'who's failed so much in her responsibility towards her children that she regularly offers herself to a butcher in exchange for offal.'

Karamella was stung to the quick.

'Liar!' she screeched.

'Do you want me to prove it?'

'Yes prove it! Prove it now! Prove it here!'

Karamella's hands had at last left her hips and the arms hung heavy and dimpled at her sides like blackened hams. The hands were clenched and they looked ridiculous, such disproportionately small appendages to the arms they were. They were dimpled with fat.

Maria looked at the hands, then at the belly, then she laughed.

'What are you laughing at?' Karamella said belligerently.

'At you,' Maria said pointedly, 'I wonder whether your husband has an easy time mounting you, what with that garbage mound of a belly you keep pushing around like a dung-beetle. No wonder he looks for tastier flesh elsewhere.'

'How dare you say such things in the presence of my son? I will kill you today. Maria, you bitch!' She waddled forward, raising he hands. At least *that* has had the desired effect, thought Maria.

'Come on', Maria encouraged her. 'Yes, come if you're not a coward.' She patted the spot just below her belly. 'There's nothing to fear here. We're both people who have to squat in order to urinate. so come on if fear isn't withering your thing!'

Karamella had stopped, wondering about the wisdom advancing of farther since this 'drunken' woman was encouraging her so vehemently. Karamella's uncertainty was what suddenly decided Maria, who now stepped confidently up to Karamella, worked up a little saliva in her mouth, and spat full on Karamella's face. She followed this up with a crackling slap squarely on the mouth. Karamella's hands flew up, one to the spot where the spittle had landed, the other to the mouth, almost simultaneously, as she stepped back instinctively, recoiling from the slap. Her son fled and halted a few metres away to await further developments. Apire and Betty, who had been inside the house, came running out onto the verandah. A number of people who had been standing at a distance from the quarrelling women, scattered and whispering excitedly but refusing resolutely to intervene, now drew closer.

Maria stepped forward, her right hand shot up, then her fingers, spread and crooked, raked down Karamella's left cheek, vicious like eagles' talons, leaving in their wake a set of raw scores. Karamella had rallied by this time and so she plunged forward blindly, her fat arms going round Maria, gripping her tightly as Karamella tried to wrestle her down to the ground. Maria's head reared back, the eyes maniacal, then shot forward and soon buried itself into one of her adversary's pulpy breasts. Karamella gave a shriek of pain as her arms jerked away from Maria's body, swinging back behind her like those of a soldier standing to attention, then forward and up in an effort to wrest Maria's face from where it lay buried.

That was the moment Karamella's heel hit a round stone and she rocked, stumbled, then went down, landing on her back with a thud amid a great billowing of skirt and underclothes and a thrashing of baobab legs. Maria's face was still planted on her breast, worrying it with vicious shakes of her head like a skinny mongrel clinging to the breast of a pregnant saddleback sow. The white spots on the white and black polka-dot blouse were turning crimson where Maria's teeth had sunk in.

Karamella's baby-like hands at first tried to prise Maria's head away from her injured breast, as she alternately shrieked and grunted in agony, then she transferred them to Maria's back where they began to thump away in slow, heavy beats, her legs kicking up from her all the time, making an ineffectual effort to get Maria off her stomach.

'Serves her right. She's a bully,' someone remarked.

'Even if she was a bully, Maria's son had no business breaking her kid's head?' somebody retorted.

'Turn her over and smother her, you bitch! What is all that bulk you carry around for?' a third person shouted.

Karamella's son forced his way through the spectators and hurled a stone at Maria's back. Apire and Betty crashed into the circle where the women were fighting and retaliated by kicking Karamella's legs. Hands reached out from among the crowd and flung all three of them out of the circle.

That was when Drum Major appeared. Nobody knew his real name, for he possessed a variety of names. Nobody knew where he had originally come from either, since he was fluent in a number of languages, nor how old he was. What everybody knew, however, was that this wiry old man with the back as straight as a goal post was a friend of Maria's, someone with whom she occasionally split a bottle.

Drum Major tumbled into the circle brandishing his famous *poo* walking stick which had a brass door knob for a handle. He began to hop and caper youthfully around the fighting women, cheering them on. Then he slowed down and started stalking, twirling the walking stick in front of him raptly, twitching it with sudden twists of his wrists so that it looked like a nervous cat's tail. The other spectators now watched him in addition to the scrapping women.

With a supreme effort, Karamella arched up her blubbery belly and heaved, flipping Maria over like a *chapati*. Maria rolled away in a flurry of dusty *gomesi* and came up short against unyielding legs.

She struggled up and faced Karamella who was advancing on her.

'I will teach you a lesson today,' Karamella panted, 'a lesson you'll never forget.'

She reached out for Maria who simply sank her teeth in her dimpled arm. She shrieked as she began to pummel Maria's head with her free hand.

The spectators, feeling enough was enough, intervened at this point and pulled the women apart, with Maria's teeth having to be prised from Karamella's arm, where they had stuck with python-like tenacity. The two women fell back, exhausted, pellets of blood slowly swelling up where Maria's teeth had gone in, then dripping like a slow drizzle onto the yellow sand.

Maria was hysterical, crying and laughing at the same time, cackling witch-like laughter that made some of the spectators step back in fear.

'You will tell me tomorrow,' she gasped, 'who taught who a lesson.'

'Don't you think this is the end. This time you took me unawares, next time it's going to be real war!' Karamella was pathetically out of breath, drawing out each word painfully, 'Then I'll teach you to respect women who didn't kill their husbands.'

'You ugly lover of an offal-seller,' Maria said struggling weakly to free herself. 'Leave me, leave me people, so that I show this piece of scum that I'm not somebody to fool around with.'

They had been dragged away in different directions while still hurling abuse at each other, protesting feebly in a manner the crowd thought was just empty posturing.

The following day, Maria had been arrested by the police and locked up for ten hours, but Betty had been able to scrape together enough money to secure her release before nightfall. Karamella had insisted that the bills for treating the injuries inflicted on her son's head and on her own body be footed by Maria, also that Maria pay damages. Betty had found the money promptly and the family had had to go without sauce for two days.

Karamella and Maria had gone on to become very good friend and were often to be seen together laughing and gossiping about other women.

Apire had continued to respect Betty and looked to her for guidance even after he joined secondary school. It was one of the best schools in the district and there was no need for Apire to pay school fees since he had been awarded a bursary.

During his first vacation from secondary school, Apire had built a wheelbarrow out of some timber he had unearthed from beneath a stack of old corrugated iron sheets in the tool store. He had borrowed some money from Betty – it was he who had insisted that the money be lent, not given – to buy some nails and wood glue. He had carved the wheel from a piece of wood he had sawn off the top of a stump. He had drilled a hole through the centre of the wheel, which looked rather crude but was sturdy, and that was what mattered to Apire.

He had wound a strip of rubber cut out of an old car tyre around the wheel, tacking it firmly down with one-inch nails.

That was when he had begun to make money for himself. It wasn't much but it was something. He began to hire the wheelbarrow out to professional wheelbarrow pushers, most of whom didn't earn enough money to have such wheelbarrows made for them, or couldn't save enough, or simply didn't care enough to own one. For the first time in his life, he could buy whatever little things he required by himself. Later, after he had paid off Betty's loan, he found himself in a position to buy even brand-new shoes and clothes. He felt proud!

Then the miracle had happened.

One morning, while he, his mother and Betty were seated on the front porch, his mother as usual with her mind wandering only God knew where, and he and Betty talking quietly about unimportant things, they had come across. They were four young people on four light Scandinavian-made bicycles with silvery-green frames and silver mudguards, bikes which had curved orange glass reflectors fitted to their spokes. They brought one guitar and six Bibles with them.

Acaye, who had been playing with silver coins, aiming carefully and then tossing them towards a shallow hole he had dug in the forecourt, trying as hard as he could to get the coins to land in the hole but frequently failing, looked up, puzzled.

The three young men and one young woman, who were all smartly dressed, the men in dark-blue blazers and matching trousers and the woman in a beautifully cut sombre-grey one-piece suit, looked very impressive. They dismounted and, after greeting Maria and her children, stood around holding the bicycles, evidently waiting to be invited. The first person to act was Betty. Wily girl that she had become she believed this was an opportunity to be taken full advantage of. She got up, directed Apire and Acaye to take the bicycles to the back of the house and park them there, then she invited the visitors inside the house, where she offered them seats.

Betty knew intuitively that if these young people didn't succeed in getting Maria to stop drinking and pitying herself, then nothing an earth would. Maria was so far gone in her addiction to *waragi* that she had become only a faint, barely recognisable shadow of her former self. Maria was still out there, Betty knew, sitting slouched against one of the wrought-iron roof supports like a discarded doll.

'Mama,' she called, walking towards the outside sitting room door. Then she stood framed in the doorway, 'Mama.'

Maria pretended not to have heard.

'Mama, are you listening?' Still no visible reaction from Maria, but Betty went on just the same. 'Mama, I'm asking you to come in and listen to these young people. And if you refuse, don't you ever ask me for money again.'

Betty had lots of leverage with her mother and she knew it. Maria looked up at Betty, turning half around in the process, her eyes bleary and vacuous. She was still sober but had a bad hangover.

'Betty,' she said quietly, 'if you think I'll go in there to listen to the pigswill those people are bound to spew, simply because of your dirty money, I think you're grossly mistaken. I've always hated *Balokole* and I'm certainly not going to be expected to begin liking them at this late hour.'

She reached down, snapped off a piece of grass straggling against the edge of the verandah, and began to calmly pick her teeth with it.

'Is this the way you used to behave even when Dad was alive Mama? Refusing to talk to visitors, even when they are the hated *Balokole*? Not even bothering to greet them? Surely, Mama, I should have expected you to be a lot more courteous than that!'

Maria's head snapped around. She looked steadily at her daughter. One-love against Maria, Betty thought.

'Betty,' she said, 'if I have to come into the house while those fools are still there, then I'll enter through the back door, and stay put in the kitchen making tea for them.'

Betty scowled, swung the door shut with a deafening bang, then she marched right through the sitting-room into the kitchen beyond, only muttering 'wait' to the four youths as they swivelled round in unison to stare in surprise at her disappearing anger-stiffened back.

Betty marched back to the sitting-room presently, snuffling, with a handkerchief hovering around her teary eyes.

'That woman out there,' she said, jerking her thumb angrily towards the outside door, 'is my mother. She's a widow, a drunkard and worse. She's hurting inside, killing herself with self-pity, but is not willing to accept a helping hand. Please do something for her, do something?'

'Do not let anger hold sway over your heart, sister,' one of the men said. 'We are all sinners in one way or another.'

'What should I do, then? She cannot listen to the voice of reason! She will not be persuaded to come in here and listen to you people.'

'Do not worry yourself, sister.' It was the young woman speaking. 'She will come to the Lord Jesus when the time is right.'

'No time is ever going to be righter for her than this moment, while you're still here! Because the moment your backs are turned, she's going to steal my money and go off to drink!"

Now if there was one thing that set Maria apart from the majority of self-pitying humanity, it was that she still possessed vestiges of pride. When she heard Betty accusing her of theft before total strangers, she got up, dusted the seat of her dress, shuffled up to the door and yanked it open.

'Betty,' she called, standing framed in the doorway, her bony knuckles on her hips, 'don't ever try to make me look cheap before strangers, even if they think they're saved. Because I might be tempted to order them out of the house my own husband built!"

The *Balokole* switched their attention to Betty.

'Your husband might have built the house, but I happen to be the current breadwinner. And your husband that was, also happens to have been my father.'

For a moment Maria looked uncertain as to what to do. Then she shambled off to the kitchen.

'Start up a song,' Betty whispered to the young people, "and make full use of the guitar. I know my mother loves music, of whatever variety.'

She followed Maria into the kitchen. One of the *Balokole* took the guitar out of its case and they all launched into 'I'm so glad that Jesus set me free' with gusto. They finished the song with a flourish and nervous silence descended on the room.

Betty's head poked out of the kitchen doorway: 'Keep singing while we prepare the tea. And do not stop until we bring it over.' They struck up another tune, fast and jaunty like American country music, and they rocked in their seats in time with the music.

A few moments later, Maria came in carrying a tray of black tea and buttered bread – Apire had put up the money for the bread and butter – while Betty followed with a jug of water and a large bowl for the young people to wash their hands in. Maria placed the tray on a small coffee table, drew up a larger table towards the visitors, then carefully transferred the tray to it. After that she retired to a cane chair that was stationed farthest from the *Balokole*, in a fairly dark corner of the sitting-room.

The young people said a short prayer then fell to. As they ate, Maria closely watched them from her nook. Betty was seated at the table with them, chatting happily away.

If there was one thing you could say about these four *Balokole*, mused Maria, it was they seemed genuinely happy. Plus, they were not shabby like many of the people their age whom she saw scurrying around here, idle and disorderly and bored and aimless and lacking ambition. Plus, they seemed to be very responsible and serious, especially that grey-suited girl. I should be very proud of her if she were my daughter. Betty is good too, of course, kind and diligent and industrious and neat and not crazy about men, but she's only a girl yet. Who knows how she will turn out when she becomes a young woman? A smile flitted across Maria's face.

The young lady noticed the smile with eyes scrutinising furtively from under long eyelashes. She noticed the warm smile and told herself inwardly: 'Good!'

On finishing tea, the *Balokole* immediately struck up another tune, standing this time, the guitar strumming away joyously, the lady singing with rapture, her eyes closed and Betty joining in, clapping and stamping and swaying with them.

Maria still sat, watching from her shadowy nook, deeply moved but not wanting it to show. Towards the middle of the song that followed, Maria had begun to clap her hands in accompaniment. Also to rock from side to side in her chair. When the song ended, she requested a repeat.

When the song started up again, Maria levered herself up out of the cane chair, walking as if in a trance to where the young people were. She knelt down and patiently waited with bowed head for the song to come to an end. Then she spoke.

'My children,' she said, 'I know I should not be kneeling before you like this, since my own daughter is here among you. But what she said about me is true. I am sick of myself and I need your help. Please do something about my troubles.'

The young people had all prayed over, for and with her, and before departing had extracted a promise from her to begin attending Sunday services at their chapel situated about two kilometres away. They had also left two Bibles - one in English and the other in the local language - with Maria.

As the *Balokole* left, they were overjoyed about how easy it had been to save Maria, for their evangelistic mission was only rarely blessed with victory. They told Betty about the time they had gone to the home of another drunkard and found him imbibing *waragi*, though he was already perceptibly drunk. When they had told him that he was committing a very serious sin drinking that 'poison', he had laughed wildly and asked them what he should be expected to do on a Saturday morning.

'Do something useful,' they had urged.

'Like what?' he had challenged them, and to their consternation, had lit a Crown Bird cigarette.

'Go to your farm, work at your sewing machine, anything other than taking this foul drink.'

'I'd suppose Jesus himself wouldn't have held such an opinion. Otherwise he couldn't have changed water into wine at that wedding in Emmaus. Or is it Antioch?'

'Cana,' he had been corrected.

'Cana,' he had repeated and taken a puff on his cigarette and exhaled the smoke in a blooming cloud, with his mouth rakishly twisted to one side.

'But wine isn't strong. And it's a much healthier drink than this awful stuff you're so fond of. I believe that's why wine is used in church.'

'Would you drink wine if I offered it to you? If I could afford it?'

'No. It is still an alcoholic drink, however little the amount of alcohol it contains.'

'So you believe all those priests who take it during the Eucharist are sinners?'

'We don't have any Eucharist, so we don't take it.'

'You haven't answered my question. Those priests, Catholic and Protestant, who take it during Mass, are they sinners or aren't they?"

'They are sinners.'

'So Jesus is a sinner, too, for causing those people at the marriage celebration to drink wine. He ought to have left them to drink water.'

'No, he didn't cause them to drink the wine. He only changed the water into wine and left it at that.'

'Thus tempting them to drink. You will remember he was actually requested to work that miracle, something he proceeded to do willingly and happily. Or did he only intend to show off his powers?'

'No, not that. But the stuff you're drinking will ruin your health.'

'Just as the tea you drink excessively will surely ruin your health. In any case, God endowed me with a free will, and it therefore is up to me to decide what's good and what's bad.'

'Even smoking is good for you?'

'I don't remember reading anything about smoking or tobacco in the Bible.'

The young *Balokole* hadn't left it at that, but had continued badgering him until one day he had slammed the wooden door of his decrepit grass-thatched dwelling in their faces. Then they had left him alone.

But for this woman, Maria, it had been different, perhaps even a bit too easy.

Maria had continued drinking only up to the first Saturday following her conversion. When she had come back from Church service on the Sunday, she had become a new person. Whatever had happened to her at that service nobody knew, but she had seemed imbued with a fanatical will to fight her addiction and to clean up her life. Nobody was sure whether she would win.

VII

Jean-Paul Tchicaya had turned up in their classroom one morning and beckoned to them to follow him to the French room – without speaking. They had wondered whether he was dumb. The moment they were settled, he had said something including a word which sounded like 'appel' and then had proceeded to write his name in both block capitals and small letters on the blackboard:

JEAN-PAUL
DESIRE TCHICAYA
Jean-Paul Desire Tchicaya

The students had wondered how an ordinary mortal could be expected to pronounce the 'tch' combination of letters. But the teacher had got his tongue around them, and they had sounded charming!

Then he had gone on to say something like 'kilililidwi' and had written the date on the chalkboard:

Lundi 23 janvier 19 -,

As they tried to puzzle out what it was all about, the teacher had gone into an adjoining room and brought out a square expanse of some rough cloth stretched between borders of timber, hung it up on a nail next to the chalkboard and begun to stick pictures on it, each time saying something and asking them to repeat it. After waiting in vain for the teacher to begin using English, Apire had put up his hand and the teacher had responded with what Apire thought was 'we' while nodding.

Apire believed the nodding meant he had been given permission to Speak.

'Excuse me, sir,' Apire had said, 'could you please...'

The teacher hadn't even waited for him to finish, but had uttered a series of froglike sounds and pointed to a strip of manila paper pasted to the wall above the chalkboard. What was scrawled on the paper with a marker read:

Ici on parle français!

Apire suspected that he wasn't going to like this man at all, nor the subject. Yet they had been told French was compulsory during the first two years of secondary school! Surely the person who had made that decision should be arrested and hanged feet-first!

Voici un crayon
Un crayon noir

Where had he seen this man before? He must have seen him before, and not just once... somewhere... if not in the flesh, then it must be his picture...

Jacques prend une galette.

Now what was he saying about 'gullet'? So they had 'gullet' in French also? Perhaps he was going to like the language after all!

Oui, la galette est bonne!

That 'we' again... But the man looked so much like somebody he had known by sight for some time... Wasn't he... then the resemblance hit him like a typhoon. Yes, Tabu Ley, he looked so much like the picture of Tabu Ley that he had seen inside the plastic case of a music cassette tape he had noticed in a shop window some time back... Tabu Ley the Zairean musician! Yes, this teacher with the funny name looked so much like that musician! Tabu Ley must have looked exactly like this teacher clowning before us when he had been a young man. Apire decided he would call the teacher 'Tabu Ley' henceforth!

'Tabu Ley' was heading straight for Apire's desk, croaking something incomprehensible and looking quite angry. On reaching him, 'Tabu Ley' went on croaking while pointing to the entrance door of the French room. Apire understood the message, got up and went out. He never attended any French lesson again.

Though Apire loathed French and its teacher, he liked most of the other subjects – liked them very much in fact – and he did work at them. He was always among the first to hand in his assignments, which were generally of a high standard.

His problem was, however, of a different kind. He seemed to be in a dark mood much of the time, preferred to keep aloof from both students and teachers, and often spoke to them only when spoken to. He seemed to be living in a world all his own, wholly self-sufficient, never soliciting any assistance from anybody, most times even refusing to accept such assistance when offered.

Another problem was his strong-headedness, such as when he had decided to drop French and "Tabu Ley" had reported him to the Headmaster.

'Apire,' the Headmaster had said, 'I can see from the recommendation you brought from your former primary school that you have been a very hard-working, obedient and polite boy. You are also intelligent, very intelligent. Now - I believe this is something you are already aware of - in this school when you are in S.1 or S.2, you must do all the subjects taught in those classes. 'Is that clear?'

'Yes sir.' His face was inscrutable but his sitting posture connoted boredom of the will-you-finish-and-let-me-go variety.

'You are in the best stream in your year. That means you are only one of the many brilliant and very diligent students. The members of B and C streams look at you with envy, and many of them are prepared to do everything they can to displace you. That implies you are at a serious disadvantage, taking one subject less than the rest of the class. That means every term you will be 100 marks short even before your exams are marked. Are you aware that this is a very serious state of affairs?'

'Yes sir,' Apire said, yawning.

What's wrong with this boy with the sad eyes and who looked unconcerned about the implications of what he's done, the Headmaster thought.

'First of all, I am punishing you for being insolent to a teacher by refusing to attend his lessons. After that, I shall ask Mr. Tchicaya to make sure that you at least put in an appearance at all his lessons. Is that understood?'

'Yes sir.' He looked the Headmaster straight in the face, his eyes bilious like those of a snake.

He had been directed to go with the office messenger, to whom the Headmaster had given a handwritten note, to the school quartermaster who had the freedom to mete out whatever punishment he thought fit. The quartermaster had given him a hoe and a mattock and led him to a big anthill and told him to bring it level with the ground and then look for the termite queen and take it to him in his office. It had taken Apire all of five days to do the difficult job. When he had finished it, his palms were a mass of painful blisters. He had turned away fellow students who had offered to help, telling them sullenly: 'Don't bother,' and staring balefully at those who insisted.

On the fifth day, when he had flattened the anthill and dug up the three-inch-long termite queen which he had found lying mottled and fat and dimpled and unconcerned within its clay enclosure, he had reported to the quartermaster. He had gone up to the tools store where he had found the quartermaster sorting through some tractor spares, placed the hoe and mattock down on the floor, almost dropped them in fact, then he had spoken.

'Excuse me sir, I've finished.'

'Finished what?' the quartermaster had asked. 'Oh, you're the boy who hates French! Now where's the beautiful termite queen?'

The tone was light and bantering, and that had set Apire aflame. He had been holding the queen in his hand, shrouded in leaves. He dropped it on the quartermaster's desk and turned to leave.

'Now, wait a moment,' the quartermaster said, holding up a palm dark with sump oil. 'I happen to have forgotten your name. What did you say it was?'

'Apire, Francis Apire. Anything else?' He left out the 'sir' deliberately.

'No, you may go,' said the quartermaster, who began whistling a popular dance tune immediately after.

That permission had, however, not been necessary, for Apire had already started out on hearing the 'no'. He was more determined than ever to skip all French lessons.

For the whole of that week and the following week, Apire did not attend a single French lesson, though he constantly lounged outside the French room as the lessons were going on, insolent, challenging trying to provoke. 'Tabu Ley' had, however, decided the punishment, Apire had been given was enough to have made any sensible person behave, and thought, it seemed, that if this foolish boy had decided he didn't want to have anything to do with French, well, it was no skin off his Francophone nose. So Jean-Paul Tchicaya had let sleeping dogs lie.

Fortunately for Apire, before the term came to an end, the French teacher had left. Nobody could say with any amount of certainty where he had gone, but rumour had it that he had landed a job with the embassy of his home country in the City.

Throughout his School Certificate course, Apire never had a single intimate friend. True, he had begun to talk to people more frequently now, but still they felt he was keeping them at arm's length, not wanting them to get really close to him, silently snubbing those who tried to do so in his peculiar chilly and sullen way.

Whenever he went around the school premises, therefore, the air almost crackled with hostility, or became weighted with heavy indifference towards him. What compounded the animosity and apathy towards Apire was the fact that his school work was exceptionally good so it was assumed by both his fellow students and some of his teachers that the cold disdain he was carried around with him was simply some kind of intellectual snobbery.

Apire, however, didn't seem to mind. If he wasn't exactly insulated from the unfriendliness around him, he didn't show he was aware of it. In fact he seemed to thrive on what to many – if not most people – would have been a stifling atmosphere.

He passed his O-levels with flying colours and went back to the same school for his Higher School Certificate course.

Now there happened to be an Economics teacher of Form Five nicknamed Turkey. Whoever had given him that name must have been singularly devoid of imagination. It is true Turkey was fond of women, in fact he was crazy about them and chased after them with a fervour that would have made any Mujaheddin seem like a heretic. But he didn't go after them with the fan-tailed arrogance and style of a turkey cock. He whined and pleaded with them, without any decorum at all, almost crawling on his belly, slavering, promising them things everybody knew he couldn't afford, and hardly ever scored any successes. The women despised him, and laughed at his antics behind his back.

Moreover, Turkey pitied himself. Not secretly but openly, so that his Economics classes sometimes degenerated into a forum for sounding off on his private woes. Apire despised and hated him, finding him barely tolerable.

One day, during an early-morning lesson, Turkey had shuffled in, slovenly as usual, red-eyed and slouched like a bush hat, and had begun to teach them about "Labour and Wages". He would have made a very interesting talker but for the quality of his voice, which frequently had the effect of setting one's teeth on edge. It cracked shrilly one moment, whispered dully the next, becoming almost inaudible, then rose to a high falsetto, plummeting after that to a boring drone. The bugger doesn't seem to have made any effort at all to train his voice, thought Apire. He had just learnt the word 'bugger', and it thrilled him to use it.

Suddenly, as he usually did, Turkey had veered off "Labour and Wages" and was now squeaking along about how rash and foolish it was for a man to set up his woman in business, women could never be trusted, they were all the same, whether illiterate or holding a PhD, they were scatterbrained and treacherous and childish and fickle.

'Do you know,' Turkey was saying now, 'that I was once married? This woman was very beautiful and I simply adored the ground on which she walked. Now d'you know what she went and did to me?'

'We're not interested, sir,' interjected Apire, thinking, enough is enough, sir, if somebody doesn't try to stop you now, you're going to waste the whole of this remaining hour babbling about this woman who went and did something really nasty to you!

'...teaching you!' Turkey had been speaking, but Apire had caught only the tail-end of what he had said.

Apire nudged his neighbour and whispered, 'What did Turkey say?'

He was told. Apire looked back at Turkey.

'I am repeating – and this is the last time I'm asking - who is it said we're not interested? If none of you is willing to point out the culprit, then this is the last time I'm teaching you, depend upon it. His voice was dark with menace. 'Apire, let's hope it's not you.'

So you knew after all, thought Apire.

'Yes sir!' Apire admitted, fearless, 'It's I who said it.'

'Now what exactly did you mean you're not interested?' He said it low and soft and slow, and it was pregnant with muted threat.

'I meant, sir,' Apire was doing his best to sound polite, 'that perhaps an effort should be made-er-to teach us Economics throughout the time allocated for it.'

Nobody moved. Somebody coughed in the back of the class, sounding almost guilty and apologetic.

'Apire,' the teacher was moving in his direction, his hands on his hips, 'I didn't spend three years at university and nine months in teacher training so that I could later be insulted by my students.' Turkey looked pained and pathetic. 'Some of you seem to come from families in which very little respect is accorded to the parents. Apire, if I'd been your father, would you have tried to remind me about what you imagine is my duty?'

'I have no father, sir, he died ...'

'Stand up when I'm speaking to you!'

The words and hand lashed out simultaneously. Apire's ears buzzed and he felt his head swell with shame. There was a salty taste in his mouth.

'Now get out of my class!' Turkey rapped out and headed for the entrance door of the Senior Chemistry Laboratory in which they were, for once walking erect and dignified.

When later Apire thought back to the incident, he couldn't understand what had come over him. His fellow students were shocked by the violence of his reaction, for though they suspected simply that deep down he was a very angry youth, they never thought him inclined towards physical violence.

Apire had got down slowly from the lab stool on which he had been sitting, shifted slightly, putting first one foot, then the other, on the floor, then he had come out from behind the long bench into the centre aisle. As he shuffled towards the entrance door, his face was dark and convulsed with the kind of raging fury he hadn't felt for a long time, but still he wasn't thinking of hitting Turkey. No, he had not thought of hitting Turkey at all!

Turkey, on the other hand, thought that all those shifting muscles on Apire's face were only a reflection of the shame and embarrassment he must be feeling about being slapped in the presence of his fellow students. So he replaced his hands on his hips and stared smugly at Apire as he moved towards the door to give the impression that once he set out to do a job, he followed it through to the end. He pulled the door open and held it for Apire to pass through it and out. His right hand rested lightly on the doorknob.

When Apire reached Turkey, all the control he had marshalled simply snapped. His right hand jerked upward and connected with Turkey's chin, taking Turkey by storm. Turkey's right hand came off the doorknob and both his hands shot up in an attempt to shield his face. Apire went wild, his stout figure a whirl of motion, jabbing, kicking, even butting Turky's nose with his forehead. Twin streams of crimson blood gushed out of the teacher's nostrils.

The students, taken unawares, had at first been stunned into inaction. But when they saw blood squirting from Turkey's lowered face, they panicked, each student making a dash for the only other door, stampeding, some even injuring themselves in the process, and all this amidst a noisy dragging of lab stools and breakage of some pieces of lab equipment. Nobody tried to stop Apire or to watch the rest of the confrontation.

The tussle caused such a commotion in the school that all the lessons that had been in progress at that particular moment were interrupted, with students and teachers spilling out of classrooms and the staffroom and dashing to the Senior Chemistry Lab.

Except the Headmaster, who summoned his office messenger and asked him to find out what all the noise was about. On being informed about what had taken place, the Headmaster called the school watchmen and directed them to arrest Apire. When the watchmen had turned and left his office, he picked up the phone and rang the local police station.

'Hullo,' he said, 'this is the Headmaster of St. Matthew's College.'

'Headmaster,' the officer on the other end of the line sounded bored, 'is there any way in which we could be of assistance to you?'

Why can't some people learn to be brief? thought the Headmaster. 'Yes,' he said, 'one of my senior students has run amok, seems to be a mental case. From the information I have received so far, he seems to have broken the nose of one of my staff. I am having him arrested by the school *askaris* now. Could you come over and take him to the station?'

The policeman smelt the possibility of making a little money and perked up a bit. 'Transport?' he said, adding unnecessarily, 'You know, here we have only one Landrover and it is monopolised by the DPC.'

'I know, I'm sending the school truck over.'

'School truck?' the officer sounded disappointed. 'Are you aware that this job is going to interfere with my breakfast.'

'Just grab another officer and come over!' the Headmaster sounded peremptory. 'I know what to do for hungry cops.'

'Good of you!' the officer sounded very eager.

The Headmaster gently replaced the phone and chuckled. The cops came armed with sub-machine guns, bundled Apire into the school lorry and perched on the tail-board with their guns trained on him. When they reached the station, Apire was shepherded into a damp foul-smelling cell and penned up there with a huge lock.

After five days of uncomfortable solitude in his cell, Apire was set free from gaol and expelled from school. That marked the end of his formal education.

At the time of Apire's expulsion, his family had already moved to the countryside, for life in town had become almost impossible, it being so expensive. Now if there was one thing Apire had never contemplated doing, it was settling down in the country with its petty jealousies and malicious rumours and overdrinking and the inability of most country folk to grasp even the simplest concepts or react rationally to situations he considered not worth getting all heated up about.

Moreover, though at this time his interest in girls was peaking, he found country girls singularly silly, crude, shallow, unimaginative and inelegant. And they didn't have any fashion sense either. At one point you might find them all wearing the same type of dress. He particularly hated the kind of frock nicknamed 'capsule' from the way it looked like a medicine capsule; for instance, it could have a yellow top, red waist and yellow skirt. When the girls wore the 'capsules' to market or to church, they looked to him like batches of marching medicine bottles.

Then there was Flo and the baby. Their affair had been going on for some time and Flo had become pregnant and given birth to a baby boy. He didn't see how it was going to be possible for him to look after her and the child if he didn't get a job. Farming wasn't quite in his line; nor was business if he had to operate from the village. In any case where would the capital come from?

He walked the city streets looking for a job – in government offices, in parastatals, in private firms, everywhere – until the soles of his shoes – the only pair he possessed – were completely worn out. Just when he was about to give up, and was on the verge of choosing between robbery and suicide, he landed a job as a sales assistant.

Mattattical Popat, Apire's employer, was a tall, muscular Indian with shaggy eyebrows and an even shaggier beard who loved two things: glowering at people and smoking marijuana. His customary mode of address for his black employees was 'dirty African' and he seemed to enjoy hitting people with his elbows.

He also enjoyed giving orders that had nothing to do whatsoever with what you were made to understand would be your duties the day you were offered a job at Sunshine Importers, Ltd. In this way, as a sales assistant, you would find yourself being commanded one hot afternoon to go out and help offload a truck load of cement newly arrived from Mombasa, or hoes from China, or bicycles from India. After some time, Apire knew that this wasn't a job he was going to stay in for very long, so he stuck to it just long enough to complete his training as a driver-mechanic, which training he received on his off days and during the night. He completed the training in motor mechanics in exactly one year and immediately bade farewell to Sunshine Importers.

He wasn't long in finding another job, and it was partly because in the course of his employment by Sunshine Importers he had established a few useful connections. Also, he was in possession of forged documents claiming he had three years' experience as a driver. As a result, during the next fourteen months he worked for a middle-aged high-ranking officer in the Ministry of Agriculture who, in addition to the official Isuzu Trooper, owned a double-cabin Toyota pick-up and a Ford hatchback. Apire's responsibilities included taking the official's children to school and bringing them back home in the evenings, going shopping for the official's family, taking the official's wife, Sharon, to such places as hairdressing salons and women's rights meetings and fundraising functions, as well as going on sundry errands.

And had it not been for Sharon, he would have kept his driver's job a lot longer than he actually did. His boss loved him the way he would have loved his own son, and he suspected one reason was that he treated the boss' grown-up daughters the way few young drivers did – he gave them a wide berth. But the problem had been Sharon.

First, there was the way she dressed and wore makeup. At first he had been shocked, and later became used to it all, and later still, simply amused. Like there was that day she showed up clad in leggings and a tunic sweater that didn't descend farther than mid-thigh. He had barely noticed what she had been wearing on her feet, for all his attention had been taken up by the leggings which were packed so tight with thigh and calf that they looked like giant sausages.

Or the time he was taking them – she and three of her children – to the boss' home village in the pick-up and she turned up wearing a highly fashionable ensemble – pumps, skirt, two-in-one jacket and blouse, and a broad-brimmed hat with an artificial flower attached to one side of the brim, all of the same colour. One problem with that outfit was that it was all a violent red colour. Another problem was that Sharon didn't have the kind of head meant to carry the kind of hat she was wearing. Her head was small and oval and the crown of the hat looked just a trifle too large for it, and had it been a deep crown it would have covered not only her eyes but the bridge of her nose as well. But it happened that this was one of these dish-like hats one often sees in the windows of shops, and Sharon's made her look like World War Two British soldier; only, being ill-fitting and balancing precariously, the wide-brimmed inverted dish of a hat looked ridiculously incongruous and unprotective. To make it worse, she had plastered her lips with crimson lipstick, her cheeks with purple rouge and her eyelids with greenish eyeshade. The upshot was that she gave exactly the impression she seemed to be fighting so desperately: a tired, sickly, overweight woman who was evidently older than her husband. Apire wondered whether it was his small-town and rural upbringing that made him look at Sharon the way he did.

Second, Sharon never seemed able to discuss serious things maturely and she spoke in a small-girl voice that made her own teenage daughters sound like old women.

'D'you know I've got a daughter in Ciskei?' she asked Apire. Apire knew but pretended he didn't. He shifted the gear lever. 'I hope you know where Ciskei is?' she smirked. Apire again pretended ignorance. 'In South Africa,' she supplied, 'one of the black homelands; the so-called independent republics.'

'Bantustans,' Apire said, praying, if only I could keep her talking about those Bantustans, at least they're more interesting than these daughters who're living in them.

'So you know!' Sharon said, looking relieved.

'Yeah, read about them somewhere. Transkei and others. One called Baphu-something. Only I hadn't heard abut Ciskei yet,' he lied.

'That's where my daughter lives. I love her so much that I had her baptised Sharon too. Elizabeth Sharon. Ain't the name cute?'

Apire grunted and proceeded to yawn.

'Liz – Elizabeth that is – is living with a teacher. And out of wedlock. He eloped with her to Ciskei two years ago.'

Apire grunted again.

'The boy had just graduated from university – he's called Tom or something – and couldn't get a good job. My daughter had been a nurse for one year before this boy came along and began pumping ideas of rebellion into her head.'

In spite of himself, Apire was getting curious.

'Rebellion?' he asked.

'Yes, rebellion. She'd been very, very loyal to the family before. I had told her point blank I wasn't going to tolerate anybody less than a successful doctor or engineer or lawyer or a wealthy, educated businessman for her husband. And then one unhappy morning she comes home dragging a mere teacher behind her and insults me by saying: 'Mama, this is the man I intend to marry.' Before she tells me that, however, I look closely at him and discover he's handsome. Then I begin to wonder about his occupation. At first I think he's a company executive or a corporate lawyer or something of the kind, for he's wearing a Dior tie, Van Heusen shirt and quite an expensive D.B., something that looks like a Saville Row.'

"What's D.B.?'

'Double-breasted coat. You know, those labels matter a lot. Those are world-famous fashion trendsetters. Well, the way the young man's dressed, I get the impression he's something important. So I take my daughter aside and, all excited, I whisper into her ear, "Tell me, what is he?" and she tells me, "A teacher". I almost get a stroke. So I leave her standing there and flee to the bedroom, all hot with shame. She follows me to the bedroom to plead with me to please try to understand, she's very much in love with him and he's a very nice boy, they can and will succeed together, but I order her never to disgrace my house again by bringing that pauper with her. D'you know what she tells me? She tells me this teacher has a lot of land and they could get a loan and do a spot of farming to supplement their income. I laughed, I tell you I laughed! Mr Apire, who's got very rich out of farming?'

'Seems to me some people have,' he sounded irritated.

'Really wealthy? I doubt it. I couldn't quite see my daughter in the role of a teacher-farmer's wife. That wasn't what I had brought her up to be. And I tell her so.'

'What does she say?'

'Begs me to understand, to see sense where there's no sense. D'you know what that young man's father is?'

'A policeman?'

'Lowlier than that. A parish chief. Just imagine my daughter getting married to the son of a parish chief. What would people say? She paused a little. 'By the way, what's your father?'

'An *ogwang-gweno*,' Apire lied, thinking, let's see how you'll like that!

'What's that?'

'Local government *askari*. Never made corporal.'

'I see.' Sharon looked contemplative and just a little bit embarrassed. 'Well, I told Liz she had to stop seeing the Tom-or -something or else stop being my daughter.'

'Why? What's wrong with being a teacher's wife?'

'Man, I know how hard and risky it is to struggle to succeed in this nation. It's much, much better to get somebody who's already well-established so that he looks after you.'

'Even if he's much older than you?'

'I don't think that matters that much. In any case, older men often treat their young wives better than do men their wives' own age. ...Well, the last time I heard about Tom and my daughter, they'd fled to Ciskei,' Sharon concluded.

They hadn't talked much the rest of the way to the village.

Some time after this conversation, Sharon had begun preferring to be alone with him in the Ford and he had at first wondered about the strange light that would come into her short-sighted eyes each time he caught her eye. Then her hands had started to stray to his on the steering wheel as he drove, at times holding them for a full minute or two. Then she had taken to kneading his knees.

On one occasion she had even bought him a three-piece suit and two pairs of shoes with what she claimed was her own money.

When she had begun to look daggers at her older daughters each time she found him chatting with them, he had decided to quit his job rather than wait for her to vengefully get his boss to fire him for a misdemeanour cooked up by her. Apire had decided never to succumb to Sharon's overtures.

When he had informed his boss that he was quitting, the poor man had been incredulous, pleading with him to stay on, even promising to double his wages. But Apire had adamantly refused, claiming his father had only just died and his neighbours were already beginning to encroach on the family land. Being an only son, he said, he just had to go home and do something – what exactly, he didn't say - about that land. The boss gave him quite a substantial amount of money and wished him well, asking him to come back any time he felt like taking up a driver's job again.

After this, Apire had hunted for another job in vain, and after about six months of joblessness he had decided to go back to his home village for a little 'rest'. That was when the insurgency had started.

VIII

By now Erabu knew the difference between the frenzied stuttering of automatic small-arms fire and the spaced thudding of homemade guns. He knew that when you heard automatic weapons firing rapidly, that probably meant friends come to tackle the cattle rustlers, but still you got out of your hut to hide behind any nearby bush to ascertain if it actually was friends. You never could be very sure these days.

When you heard dully thudding reports, however, you didn't want to find out. You knew who were coming. At times you could pick up the rending crash of G3s mixed in with the thump of the homemade guns, but still there would be no rapid fire. Those rustlers surely knew how to be economical with their ammunition.

Erabu had taken to wearing his two pairs of trousers, one on top of the other, to bed. In the pockets of the trousers he wore underneath he kept his identification papers as well as all his money.

Everybody agreed the cattle raiders should be given credit for being ruthlessly systematic and thorough. They had gone through the neighbouring counties like a horde of Phillistines, killing, raping, pillaging, burning, tearing up, trampling, cutting. But fate had so far spared Erabu's county from their vicious onslaught.

Till one chilly night. Their arrival caught most of the people, including Erabu, completely off their guard. Erabu was sound asleep, with his thick, coarse blanket drawn over his head and tucked in beneath his nose and mouth. How he managed to breathe with his head muffled that way was a miracle, but still he always slept on his belly, instantly waking up the moment he turned onto his side or back and rolling over onto his face again. He wondered why he couldn't sleep on his side or back like other people.

Erabu was lying on his stomach and dreaming. He was dreaming that thousands of cattle were being driven right through their homestead, the drivers frantic and desperate, lashing out at the animals with sticks that landed with a sharp crack. The long

94

line of cattle thundered past the door of his hut, dark, fleeting, indeterminate shapes. And he could smell them. He could also hear the dull explosions of distant gunfire, which was drawing nearer.

Later, he couldn't quite figure out whether he had been dreaming, or whether what had been happening had simply penetrated his sleep-dulled senses. In which case, he would have been hearing the animals drum past and the guns explode and smelling the musty odour of the animals as they stampeded right in front of his door.

What he knew for certain was that when he became fully awake, animals were thundering past his hut and guns were going off and the smell of cattle and goats and sheep had penetrated into his hut, a smell that was rank and pungent and overpowering and which almost choked him.

And he had doubtless been taken unawares. After two months of daily going to bed in a double layer of trousers and waiting for the raiders in vain, Erabu, like many other people, had been lulled into a false sense of security. The trousers had begun to make him feel like a stuffed doll, what with the calico bedsheet and the thick, coarse blanket he covered himself with. When the rustlers came, therefore, Erabu was skimpily clad in old brief pants with much of the seat gone. Only the front could have provided any kind of effective cover for his nakedness. He rolled off his hard bed assembled from saplings and sticks and landed with a thud on the cowdung-smeared floor. He shot up and desperately reached for his trousers, both pairs of which he wisely kept on the crudely-made bedside table during the night as he slept. He grabbed up both pairs, hastily ran his palms over them feeling for the tell-tale bulges, then flung the pair with the empty pockets onto the bed. He tried getting into the trousers he was holding but only ended up with his legs going into one trouser leg.

Scared and panicking, he plumped down on the creaking bed and kicked off the garment, scooped it up, grabbed the pair on the bed, yanked free the cheap brown shirt hanging on a nail above the bed, then he dashed out with the bundle in the crook of one arm.

He thought of going to the family kraal to set the cattle free but realised such a mission wasn't possible now. The explosions were getting nearer and nearer, and to mark their progress, giant sheets of crackling flame, orange and streaked with lilac, leapt up, spastic, and crazily licked at the inky darkness.

He turned and fled in the direction he had heard the animals and their drivers take. He didn't run very far. He sought a thick stand of tall grass and burrowed himself under it.

After an eternity, when all you could hear were shots and shouts and animals lowing and mooing and bleating, when your heart almost choked you with its violent, frightened beating, an even more frightening silence descended on the village.

The raiders had grabbed what they wanted, wreaked havoc, then turned back. When dawn came, there wasn't a single one of them around.

Dawn found Erabu on his way home, hunched with fatigue, his body a mass of itches from the prickly hairs of the grass among which he had spent the night with only his bottomless briefs on. Now he was properly clad in his two pairs of trousers and the brown shirt that he had bought second-hand at the local market only a few weeks before. His feet dragged and he frequently stubbed his toes on the stone-strewn path.

A lot of shock awaited him as he headed home, and he knew it. So when he saw the blackened ruins of the grass-thatched huts with only the ragged tips of the poles sticking up above the smoke-blackened and heat-pink walls, the poles crowned with white, powdery ash or still glowing an angry crimson with burning, he didn't cry.

He didn't cry either when he proceeded to the kraal and found its entrance open and the eight hundred head of cattle gone.

He didn't cry when he visited the long grass-thatched shed that had housed the goats and sheep during the nights and found it razed to the ground. Apart from two hapless sheep that had been trapped in the conflagration and which were now shrunk and dessicated in death, there was no sign of the animals. They too had been driven away.

He didn't cry as he shuffled towards where his hut had been and reached the spot and halted, standing still with his head bowed like a pilgrim reaching holy ground only to find it irredeemably desecrated. No, Erabu didn't cry nor did he feel any heart-thumping, head-throbbing, bowel-churning anger. He only felt cold - cold and numb and dazed and empty, curiously disembodied, de-essenced.

He sought out a boulder, his mind in a swirling mist. The villagers began to drift back, silent zombies completely oblivious to their surroundings, barely conscious they were moving; ghosts which looked up at you but didn't see you, their eyes pain-glazed unseeing marbles, eyes dead and unfocussed and impenetrable beyond the pain. Only the pain was evident and palpable.

When Erabu's mind cleared, he began to think of Esina. Esina of the mellow and slanted eyes and the tilted nose. Esina of the graceful neck and arms and legs. Esina with the protruding behind and the broad hips. Esina his lover, Esina the apple of his peasant's eye filled with the images of land and crops and cattle and ox-plough. Esina that he had planned to marry in a few months' time, whom it would not be possible to marry now since his father didn't have a single animal to his name. Oh Esina - Esina - Esina! His mind went blank.

When Erabu's mother and father and sister drifted back like the others, they found him still seated on the boulder, leaning a little forward, his elbows planted on his thighs, his chin in his palms, and his eyes staring vacantly into space.

* * *

The man for whom Erabu worked in town was a middle-aged produce dealer. To look at him, one would think he was built out of thick slabs of fat draped in sleek skin. There were pockets of fat around his eyes. Rolls of fat sagged under his chin and behind his neck. There were more rolls around the waist and the junction between the upper arms and the torso. There was a shifting ball of fat around his groin. What should have been his belly was a gelatinous hillock of fat. The man was simply an overflowing mass of huge mounds of undulating fat. He stood with his hands dovetailed behind his back and smugly watched Erabu and his workmates crush stones within enclosures divided by low walls which would soon cut off one room from the other.

Erabu had at last found regular work building this huge structure which was intended to become a restaurant-bar and lodge. Before landing this job, he had engaged in hundreds of odd jobs which earned him just enough money to keep body and soul together.

He had left his home village the day after the cattle-raiders had ravaged it. He had walked away from the torched dwellings and the empty kraal and the charred remains of the sheep, determined to make a living in town. He had only his brown shirt and two pairs of trousers and meagre savings and identification papers to call his own. He had no illusions about urban life: he knew it would be tough-going for him since he didn't have any formal education worth calling by that name or any skills training, or enough money to set up in business. But he drew some sort of comfort from the little wad of banknotes he had in the pocket of his trousers. He believed the money was sufficient to tide him over the first few days of his stay in town.

On reaching town, Erabu had noticed that most of the displaced people were headed in one direction and he had followed them. He had ended up at the Rehabilitation Office. It was the first time he had heard the word 'rehabilitation' and he wondered what it meant.

In the Rehabilitation Office had been a man and two women who had asked him details about himself and noted them down. He had been given a card bearing his name, age, marital status, village of origin and other details and told: 'Go behind the building.'

'Which one?' he had asked.

'This one. There are people standing around under some trees. Join them and wait for us there.'

Some of his anxiety had left him and he had begun to feel that here were people who surely understood the plight of displaced people and sympathised with them, and would take the sharp edge off their suffering.

The man and the two women had come walking round one end of the building and halted in front of them.

'Line up!' the man had said. His manner had been brusque and he'd sounded irritated.

They had lined up. It was a long, jagged, multi-coloured queue, an intriguing mix of disparate fashions and ages and heights and builds and shapes and standing postures. A long, long queue that extended past the backyard of the Rehabilitation building and doubled back upon itself, forming an untidy U-shape. One upright of the U turned left in a sharp curve and straggled for about fifty metres. The U had grown a tail, and from the air it would have looked like a fish-hook without an eyelet.

'For today,' the man said, 'you will be given some smoked fish and maize flour. Now we want four men to help with the distribution of the fish and flour.'

Erabu had swallowed. This was a surprise! He had expected they would be issued with beans, and beans of poor quality at that, and here was this man talking of fish! He had swallowed again.

Four men had detached themselves from the queue and come forward. They had been led to the food store and had come out carrying sacks of maize flour which they had deposited on the verandah of the building.

They had then gone back in to fetch the fish which had also been packed in jute bags. They had set the bags down beside the flour and stood awkwardly around them. Erabu had done a quick count. Four bags of flour and two of fish. His eyes had slid along the queue, from head to tail. This food is certainly not going to be enough for us, he had told himself.

That day he had received half a kilo of flour and a portion of fish the size of his hand and had been told they should last for two days. Though he had felt this wasn't enough, he hadn't complained. He had carefully wrapped the flour and fish in his brown shirt.

They had then been directed to an abandoned cotton ginnery and told that was to be their camp. In one of the ginnery buildings, he had found a little free space between two walls and had made a broom and swept out the thick mound of bat guano that had accumulated there. The place had smelt like a bat-infested cave he had visited a few years before.

He had collected some dry twigs and borrowed a small battered *sufuria* and had boiled the fish and made some maize *ugali*. He had not slept that night.

When dawn had broken, he had decided he wasn't going to rely entirely on half a kilo of maize flour and a miserable piece of fish that were meant to last two days for the duration of his stay in the camp. He had thought his sojourn wouldn't be long.

When he had got up that morning, he had gone to look for work...

'Can I weed your maize garden for money?'

'No, I can do the work myself, thank you.'

'But you have some money to spare? So that I could do some other work?'

'No, certainly not.'

'You have a big cassava field. Can I weed some rows in exchange for a few tubers of cassava?'

'No, I have a lot of mouths to feed. I need all the cassava I can get.'

'Can't you spare only two tubers?'

'No.'

'Not even just one?'

'Not even that.'

'Good morning, sir,"

'Morning.'

'Is there any work going round here for people like us?'

"What kind of people are you?"

'Displaced people. Refugees. Running away from cattle rustlers.'

'What sort of work can you do?'

'Any.'

'Any? What do you mean, any?'

'Digging – carrying things – cleaning around the house.'

'Oh, I have maize grain here which has been invaded by weevils. It needs sorting and winnowing.'

'I'll do that, Sir.'

Day in, day out, it had been that way, with luck attending h' efforts on certain days, and with him being unable to secure work and thus having to spend the money he had brought with him on other days. The money hadn't lasted more than two weeks. The Civil Servants had been the worst, never wanting to part with even a single shilling.

Their rations from the Rehabilitation office had dwindled, and then had petered out.

Grunt! Grunt!

This work is hard,

Grunt!

but at least I have something to do

Grunt! Grunt! Grunt!

unlike some people with whom I came

Grunt!

to town, who go to bed hungry every other day

Grunt!

Grunt!

because they don't have anywhere

Grunt!

to earn money regularly

Grunt! Grunt!

This is difficult work, unlike farming

Grunt!

I would now be following

Grunt! Grunt!

my beautiful oxen, Lomongin, Nyerere.

Grunt! Grunt!

Or Opio and Epeju.

Grunt! Grunt!
I wonder what has happened
Grunt!
to Esina, my Esina.
Grunt! Grunt!
If only I could save some money,
Grunt! Grunt Grunt!
I would go where she's staying
Grunt!
and sneak away with her.
Grant! Grunt! Grunt!
I'm told
Grunt!
that in some parts
Grunt! Grunt!
of the country
Grunt!
raided by those thieves
Grunt! Grunt!
they've already begun to marry
Grunt!
using pigs, even piglets.
Grunt! Grunt!
'Erabu!'

Erabu almost dropped the heavy hammer. Then he recognised the voice. It was his fat employer speaking. The sight of the man always awed him. His hammer was still held frozen above his head.

'Yes sir?' Erabu answered, bringing the hammer down.

'I wanted to talk to you.'

'Yes sir?'

'I mean, come over here, so that we can talk.'

Erabu straightened up from his crouching position and shambled over to the produce dealer.

'Yesterday you talked about your father.'

'Yes sir.'

'Well, when you finish here, come to the shop. I shall advance you some money.'

'Yes sir.'

The man lumbered away towards his dark-blue Datsun pick-up. Erabu shuffled back towards his work station.

Who was it had told him that once trouble had laid siege to your house it would be almost impossible to get it to move on? Now he here was, pounding away at stones, his palms bruised and blistered, smarting with the effort of crushing the blasted stones, his back and neck a knot of pain, yet trouble wouldn't let go!

His father had arrived in town a few days before, broke and in very poor physical shape. His scrotum was bloated like one of those canvas waterbags he had so often seen dangling from the bumpers of the big Fiat trailer trucks that used to ply the trunk road running east to west right in front of their home. Only the scrotum hadn't begun to leak yet, he pondered wryly, though it was giving the poor old man hell!

He had taken his father to hospital only the day before. The Senior Medical Assistant, stocky, bald and beetle-browed, had stared oldly at them and snapped: 'We don't provide medical forms here!"

He had scrambled out of the stifling room and bought a small piece of lined paper, about half a sheet. He had rushed back, half-walking, half-running.

'Name?' the Medical Assistant had asked his father, barking.

'Malinga,' his father had answered, frightened.

'Other names?'

'Batulumayo.'

'Age?'

'I am not very sure, but should be around sixty.'

'All right, sixty. I'll put it at sixty, though you look a bit older. Where do you come from?'

Malinga had told him.

'Problem?'

Malinga had shown him the discomfiting bulge below his belly and had described what it felt like down there.

'That thing needs to be drained.' The medical man had actually used the English word 'drained' though Malinga didn't know a word of English.

'Eh?' Malinga had asked, puzzled.

'I said, that thing will have to be cut open and the fluid inside it taken out. That, however, is for later. What you need right away is an injection and a few tablets.'

They had gone from one part of the hospital to another, until they had found themselves coming back to the same place and being asked, with thinly-veiled hostility, to proceed elsewhere. Eventually, Erabu had got the message.

He knew now that what these people with the gruff voices and rude manners wanted was money. He had left the hospital and sought out his employer to explain his predicament to him.

Erabu worked hard and ate the cheapest foods. He wanted to save money. He still thought and dreamt a lot about Esina. He couldn't get rid of the images of cattle. His nose was full of their smell, and at times he caught himself walking with his arms stretched out in front of him, the hands firmly gripping the handles of an imaginary ox-plough. When it rained on the tarmacked barrenness of town, he felt homesick. He pined for the sodden squelch of mud under his bare feet as he rushed out of their now non-existent kitchen to hurriedly pluck a few ears of green maize. Pluck them while the rain slashed down and pelted his head and shoulders and water swished around his feet. Pluck them and then run back inside, awkward and ungainly, with the mud sucking at his feet, to roast the maize, crackling and exploding and aromatic, at the fireplace. A real fireplace too, formed by three biggish stones with the fire burning yellow and slow and unsteady in their midst, to bring out the best in the maize. No he didn't like this town maize which was roasted hurriedly over braziers so as to save time and charcoal. Maize that had been bought the previous day and that had gone stale and lost its sweetness. Maize that had at times overmatured and that made your head ache around the ears as you chewed it. And to make it worse, it wasn't free! Nothing in this town was free, not even water!

And the funny habits these townsfolk had! At home, when you ate meat, you ate it in big chunks served in a deep bowl that was full to the brim - full of gravy prepared with groundnut paste. You pinched off a small mound of *atapa* and moulded it into a ball with your fingers. Then you dented the ball with your thumb and scooped up some gravy with the *atapa* and ate it. You picked a hunk of the meat and bit off a mouthful and put what was left on the dinner table. Every now and then, you picked up the bowl and sipped the thick, tasty liquid.

But here in town it was all so different! Each person was given his own two little – very little – pieces of meat on a plate the size of a saucer with only a smear of gravy that one could only drag cassava or potatoes or banana or rice or whatever else across, so that what one put in one's mouth was a lot of cassava or potato or banana with only a dab of gravy on it, gravy that had a lot of oil in it to hide its meagreness. And you were expected to nibble at the two small pieces of meat like a mouse, carefully tearing off only a strand or two at a time lest the meat got finished before the meal came to an end. Wonder of all wonders, some townsfolk even ate their sauce with wheat bread! What madness! How could any sane person be expected to say he was satisfied after eating such light, porous stuff that was only meant for taking tea with!

Also the way some of these townswomen behaved! Look at Perpetua for instance. Going on as if she hadn't been married at one time, as if she was not yet thirty! And without shame too, even among people who knew her, and whom she knew knew her, such as himself.

Where on earth does a woman get the courage to survive on pieces of roast lung and maize – both as a source of money and food for herself and her son? He had seen it with his own eyes: Perpetua putting some skewered pieces of lung and a few ears of corn over a *sigiri* and skipping off to a nearby bar to do a little dancing, leaving her five-year-old son to watch over the lung and maize. Perpetua coming back to find the maize charred and the lung parched and shrivelled and brittle. Perpetua giving her son a hot slap on the mouth and picking him up by the neck and flinging him down in the dust like a rain-drenched hen, screaming all the time, even as she gave him a smart kick on the ass as if she were a Korean-trained soldier. Then picking up her son again and ordering him to eat all the pieces of lung and all the ears of maize, even those which were still raw, and the child doing so tearfully and pleading all the time, please Mama, Mama please, forgive me, pardon me just this once, I won't allow anything to burn again, I can't finish these things, eating them will make me sick. And Perpetua removing a slipper from her foot and lashing out at the boy's pate with it, screaming at him to vanish or else. The boy running away and keeping away for some time but later being spotted clinging desperately to his mother's denim skirt, clinging with both his hands, as the mother swung madly to the beat of a South African hit in the kwete bar, completely ignoring her love-starved son.

One day, three young men, one of whom he had been in primary school with, came to see Erabu. Erabu knew him very well, for the young man had gone on to secondary school and then proceeded to join the national army as an officer cadet on completing his O-level course. Later he had deserted the army. The three men painted a picture of the future that Erabu found quite attractive.

'Do you know,' said his former schoolmate, 'that we have a lot of support, even here in town? Many of the people here know what we're planning to do, but they won't go and report us to the military authorities. Why? Because they know our struggle is justified.'

'What did you say your name was?' one of the other two, the strangers, asked.

'Erabu.'

'Yes, Erabu – what we're talking about is having enough food to eat, and good food too. And having a gun as well as wearing a beautiful uniform. Also being supplied with money – dollars, plenty of dollars – by people living outside this country. At the end of it all, of course, you'll get your cattle back.'

Erabu had heard about dollars before and had wondered about them. What did they look like, these dollars about which people talked with so much awe? He had been told without dollars you couldn't buy cars or lorries, you couldn't buy motorcycles or bicycles or wheelbarrows or radios or watches or cement, nor even a single needle! Those who brought these and other things into the country just had to go looking for them armed with the dollar, or they would inevitably come back empty-handed. The dollar was that mighty.

And the young man had also mentioned cattle!

'Now those dollars,' Erabu said. 'Shall we be paid in dollars?'

'Well,' the other stranger, the one who hadn't spoken hitherto, said, 'nobody is going to pay us. Those dollars will simply be sent to us for us to do whatever we want with it. And nobody will ask questions.'

'Are you satisfied now?' Erabu's former schoolmate asked. Erabu kept quiet, thinking. He was tense and felt uncertain. He wondered whether what he had been told was the truth or whether it simply represented a ploy designed to lure him into a situation that might later turn out to be very unpleasant and difficult to get out of. He had never handled a gun before. Nor had he liked violence and had only resorted to it when some foolish boy or other had tried to get his hands on Esina. But that was the kind of fight you enjoyed, for it pitted you against someone of more or less equal strength, and it was done with slaps and punches and kicks and a little butting. It was only meant to keep intending encroachers off your turf, not to kill them. And you wanted the girl over whom you fought to hear about your physical prowess, about how you rolled your opponent in the dust, and be proud of you.

'Are you satisfied now?" Erabu was asked again.

'Will you give me some time to think?' answered Erabu.

'O.K. Until when? This evening?'

'No, tomorrow. In the morning.'

'All right, tomorrow morning then. But, remember one thing, we're not trying to force you. We want you to decide on your own.'

After telling him a few other things and reassuring him that everything would turn out all right, the three young men had left.

We want you to decide on your own, they had said, thought Erabu. Now if there had been anything fishy about the whole thing, would they have said that? Certainly they would have tried to force me to join them. And while talking they had kept their voices low, they had sounded gentle and patient and understanding, as if they simply wanted to persuade, not to coerce. We want you to decide on your own... we want you to decide on your own...

It kept singing in his head, over and over and over, like one of those moulded likenesses of the Virgin Mary that was fitted with a screw at the bottom and which tinkled a short tune when you tightened the screw. A friend had lent Erabu one such statuette one day and he had been surprised to realise it shone a frightening faint green during the night.

What choice did he have anyway? His current circumstances weren't exactly the best. Was he going to spend the rest of his youth breaking stones and pouring concrete, building other people's houses for them? Moreover, the cattle rustlers still kept ranging over the length and breadth of his county, in ever more destructive waves, for reasons best known to themselves, so that precluded the possibility of going back home, at least not in the near future anyway. To make it worse, his father and mother and sister now all depended on him, and it was no easy task looking after them. Especially the father, who was old and sick and could not work.

What those three young men had promised was the possibility of having a crack at the raiders – at least that kind of violence he would relish! And then at the end of it all, there was the near certainty of getting his hands on a few cattle. Who knows, he might even be able to marry Esina after all.

When the three young men returned the following day, Erabu had made up his mind. He left with them.

IX

The ambush had worked out well better, much, much better than they had dared to think it would turn out.

That lieutenant had been very stupid, sitting on the bonnet of the Landrover like that! Perhaps he'd thought he was in his grandmother's house.

If only the whole bunch of them could die like him, with only a little hole in one side of the head and a little crater on the other – no wasted bullets – little bleeding – and leaving behind a smart set of camouflage fatigues and brand new leather boots.

Apire was happy as he walked ahead, leading his small band of men, most of them young men in their teens and mid-twenties. Erabu, as usual, followed close on Apire's heels.

That morning they had laid an ambush for a Landrover and a four-ton truck full of soldiers and ammunition and provisions. They had been careful not to blow up the vehicles, lest they lose all the ammunition and food. The men were in desperate need of these things. He, Apire, had only twenty rounds in his magazine yet he was leader of this straggly line of men.

They had grabbed as much of the ammunition and food as they could carry. They had picked the enemy's weapons with care, choosing only the newest Kalashnikovs and Uzis and LMGs and knee mortars and leaving the rest in the vehicles. They had removed the new uniforms from the bodies of the dead soldiers and tied them up in a bundle and given them to the only survivor of the attack to carry. The uniforms would come in handy, even those riddled with bullet holes. Many of his men either didn't have uniforms at all or had uniforms which were badly frayed and threadbare and needed replacing. He himself didn't have uniform trousers.

It had been easy, almost too easy. Their courier had come riding his bicycle at breakneck speed and, even before he had leapt off the machine, had already begun to speak. He had told them there were an army Land Rover and a lorry coming up their way.

110

In a few minutes, the ambush was in place. A few minutes later, they had spotted a tell-tale trail of dust moving in their direction. The vehicles had been going fast and the drivers didn't seem to have been ready for what they so suddenly met: two big tree trunks lying right across their route.

It was Erabu who had picked off the lieutenant perched on the bonnet of the Landrover jeep with his gun angled up and forward as if he was expecting the enemy to come at him from up front. It hadn't been much of a fight.

Apire had reached the periphery of their camp – they had several, this one wasn't the one they had set up the ambush from – and his body had suddenly gone all tense. Also, there had been that tingling sensation which always warned him of danger. He dived to the ground and his men followed suit. There was something which didn't quite fit in the picture of this place which he always carried around in his mind. There was an extraneous element here, an alien presence.

It was only the thudding of his heart and the hissing of his breath – both of which sounded disproportionately loud to him – which filled his ears. There was no other sound. There was no movement either.

Then a duiker exploded from behind a thorn bush across the glade where they had intended to bivouac; it streaked up over the shrub and landed snorting in the clearing. It stood uncertain for a few moments, gave another snort, turning right, and in three giant leaps cleared the open space and vanished into the scrub.

Apire now knew there were unwelcome guests right ahead of them. Well, he wasn't going to take the risk of having himself and his men turned into stinking bushmeat at such short notice.

He beckoned to his men and began to crawl away in the direction the frightened duiker had taken, but angling off towards the right.

That was when all hell broke loose.

The bullets came sweeping from up ahead and slightly to their left, very close to the direction from which they had initially come.

For the first time in his life, Apire was really frightened. He shot up and ran. Impulsively. His legs had completely taken command. He bore right and ran stumbling among the low scrub and tufts of grass. The bullets whipped past him in a maniacal cacophony. One struck the right rolled-up sleeve of his plain green shirt, ripping a hole through it and nicking a piece of flesh. Apire ran on.

Then his mind began to work. He was running towards a swamp. They were being herded towards a swamp from which it would be difficult, nay impossible, to escape. They would get stuck there and simply be massacred. He couldn't turn back. That would mean running smack into the enemy. He angled to the left. It was beginning to be really heavy-going here – the ground was sodden. His left foot struck a clump of swamp grass and he sprawled headlong, his SMG flying away and landing ahead with a dull thud. He crawled towards it on his belly, grabbed it, picked himself up and stumbled crouching towards a thick stand of papyrus. He landed in the water with a heavy, awkward splash. He had still ended up in the swamp, but he had a place to hide, and was closer to dry land in any case.

Then he heard the all too familiar chugging. The gunship came at them with its machine guns flashing. It raked the surface of the water, sending up misty water spouts, banked right and disappeared for a moment. Then it came at them again. This time it hovered a moment, immobile like a giant fossil arrested in flight. He saw twin plumes of white smoke escape from under its stubby wings. Then he heard a whoosh. He ducked under the water.

Even with his head immersed in water, his ears could still pick up the explosion of the bombs as they landed on the dried-out part of the swamp: they sounded eerily muffled and distant, as if he was hearing them in the twilight universe of a dream. The explosions set off ripples that lapped gently against the stalks of papyrus and against his head.

He kept diving under water and coming up at discreet intervals until, after what seemed an eternity, the gunship stopped coming.

He waded among the papyrus, pushing the green, pliant stalks out of his way with his gun, until he reached the further edge of the swamp. He realised this was a very good vantage point from which to reconnoitre the dry land lying beyond, just within his reach but forbidding in its utter uninhabitedness. He couldn't see a single soul there, nor any other living creature either. He decided it wasn't safe to get out of the swamp yet.

A few minutes later, he heard a burst of automatic gunfire and a scream. It came from the open area of swamp where the chopper had concentrated its attack. He was certain that that strangled cry of agony had come from the throat of one of his men who had either been shot dead or seriously wounded. If the latter were the case, then he would most probably be captured. Their attackers must be mopping up. He hankered further down in the water, with the spot on his arm where the bullet had struck aching with a dull, throbbing pain. The bullet wound, being shallow, had bled for only a short while and then clotted.

Shall I ever have another chance to set eyes on you, mother, and you Betty, you and your diffident, even shy, husband? Shall I ever see you again, Acaye?

Oh mother, mother, brutalised and buffeted by the vagaries of life until you saw no point in continuing to abstain and took to the bottle again.

Mother battling against the traditions of the clan, refusing to be inherited like a chattel by a blood relation of our father's who had kept out of sight in our hour of need and then had popped up when Betty had completed her nurse training and got married and Acaye was in the final year of secondary school. Popped up and laid claim not only to our mother but also to some of the property left behind by our father.

Mother adamantly refusing to give Betty's bridewealth to rapacious relatives whose sons were old enough to marry but had no bridewealth to marry with. Mother incurring the wrath of the entire clan by determined refusal.

Mother, finding it virtually impossible to survive in town, moving with what was left of the family to the country.

Mother cheated and bullied by the chairperson of the district branch of the National Widows' Association.

'What are you trying to say?' his mother had asked. 'Are you suggesting that we should all contribute towards this fund which would be used for buying a grain mill and a pick-up?'

'Yes, that's what I am saying,' the chairperson had responded.

'Now, what about those cash donations from foreign countries and government that we keep hearing about? Aren't they enough to buy those things with?'

'Maria,' the chairperson had looked cool and sounded sympathetic, 'we understand your problems, I mean the problems of all of you widows. You have to struggle single-handed to raise your children, clothe them, educate them. To make it worse, sometimes you have other dependants as well. Is that right?'

'Yes.' It wasn't only Maria who had answered, but the other widows as well.

'But the Association is faced with a serious shortage of money,' she said. 'Those donations you keep hearing about over the radio are not sufficient for even our most basic needs. We need fuel for the vehicles we use to reach you people. And these vehicles have to be repaired every now and then. They also require spares. We the officials of the Association have to eat while on duty. Furthermore, when we go to the City to talk to the President of the Association we have to hire rooms in lodges and pay for other services. All this costs a lot of money. Now that means very little money is left over from the donations after we have taken care of those needs alone. I hope you understand.'

'Yes we do,' Maria had said. 'And that money which is left over... couldn't you start something with that money while you look for more money elsewhere, from other sources?'

'Which sources?'

'You should know, you are one of the people who go to the capital city to meet the President of the Association.'

A ripple of soft laughter had spread among the assembled women, starting from the chairperson. The widows were relaxed and hopeful and were making a genuine effort to understand why they would have to raise money to top up what they would receive from Government and those other obscure bodies concerned with the plight of widows nationwide.

They were also full of goodwill towards this tall, very dark woman with slender fingers and beautiful beads around her neck. They were impressed by the aura of sophistication, good breeding and authority that enveloped her. They admired and envied the intricate manner in which her hair had been braided. They also liked what she wore: the *kitenge* top with the puffed elbow-length sleeves and the ankle-length skirt that tapered downwards and that was festooned with a ruffled length of the same cloth material which cascaded from her waist down to her ankles like the catwalk round a fuel storage tank.

They wished the stilleto-heeled patent-leather shoes she had on her feet were their own.

'That is an interesting thing you said, Maria,' the chairperson had said. 'But the problem is that there are lots and lots of widows throughout the country among whom this money has to be distributed. What our branch of the Association would get might not even be enough to buy a single hoe for each one of you. And we are not likely to have access to resources of money other than those which we already have. Not in the foreseeable future anyway.'

When this woman with the overpowering presence had first been introduced to them, the widows had been very impressed right away and they had wanted to know as much as they could about her. Was she a widow? they had asked. The answer had been 'no'. Then why had she been elected chairperson and who had elected her? No, she had not been elected but appointed by the President of the National Widows' Association himself. Was she married? they had enquired. Oh yes! they had been reassured. They had been informed that she had been in exile in a neighbouring country for a number of years and, though not a widow, she had lost a son to the same regime that had made them all widows. Also she was well-educated and brave and knew a lot of English and thus was capable of representing them effectively.

'Now how much should we contribute?' one of the other widows had asked.

'Now we're getting somewhere at least. You are many and some of you are traders. I think the traders should put up a little more money than the others.'

There had been a rumble of protest from the traders but they had eventually been convinced of the need to pay more since they were likely to use the pick-up more frequently as they tended to be more mobile than the farmerfolk.

'How much does each person pay then?' It was still the same woman.

'I shall leave that to you to decide. I shall be coming back in two weeks' time to find out about what you have decided and to see how much money you have collected.'

After that, the chairperson had chatted with them about their families, politely enquiring about their children, complaining about how hard it was to secure ingredients for the finer dishes these days, talking generally about those things that are so dear to the hearts of women. Then she had left to chair other meetings of other branches of the Widows' Association.

A few months later, the widows had succeeded in collecting enough money for 'their' pick-up and grain mill. The chairperson had bought the mill and had had it installed in her home village. She had also bought the pick-up, a Mazda, and none of the widows had been afforded an opportunity even to *hire* it.

They had invited the chairperson to several of their meetings so that she could explain her strange behaviour to them but she had not responded.

They had then sent a delegation to her to find out why the mill had been installed in her home village and why they had been denied the right to use the pick-up. It was a delegation of seven women that included Maria. When they had arrived at the chairperson's home, she had courteously welcomed them and ushered them into her beautiful sitting-room, inviting them to get seated on the plush cushions of the numerous sofas. She had told them the maid would make some tea for them and to wait for her, she had urgent business to attend to, she wouldn't be long.

Then they had heard "their" Mazda start up and roar away.

When the policemen had come, the delegation had still been busy sipping their tea, thick and heavy with milk and cream and aromatic with ginger, and munching away at the chapatis and groundnuts that the maid had generously supplied them with.

A crowd had gathered to witness their arrest but nobody had raised a finger as they were bundled into the pick-up and whisked away. On reaching the police station they had been roughly shoved into a small cell and sustained on an unvaried diet of maize bread and bean soup for three days. Then they had been released and ordered to take the first bus back to their homes. They had not been asked to make statements, nor had any charges been brought against them.

They had gone home reeking of three days' accumulated sweat and with their teeth and tongues foul with the stench of stale bean soup.

After that, the widows had not ventured to pay their chairperson a visit again. They had simply decided to let sleeping dogs lie. That, however, had not stopped them from finding out more about the woman. Her husband had ditched her two years earlier owing to her numerous infidelities. Also because she couldn't give him children. The young man who had died at the hands of the State Security agents under the previous regime, and whom she claimed had been her biological son, had been somebody she and her husband had adopted from an orphanage when he was about five years old. She hadn't exactly doted on him.

Apire tried as best he could to settle down in his uncomfortable surroundings. He didn't sleep that night. He stayed alert, his gun trained on the dry expanse of land in front of him, silently sweeping to left or right in pursuit of any moving shadow but never firing. He thought he saw a lot of dark shapes slinking past – human as well as animal shapes – but they could have been figments of his fear-sharpened imagination.

But things did move among the papyrus, and they scared him. At one time something splashed heavily in the water, to his left, and set his heart pounding, the thumping of the heart scaring him even more. At another moment, there was a flurry of wings and a tinkly whoosh on the water. He thought perhaps it was a lily trotter, but hadn't he been told that those birds never moved about at night, that that was the time they bedded down, just like human beings?

There was, however, one reality which foisted itself on him in all its ravenous relentlessness: the presence of mosquitoes, mosquitoes big and fat which burst with a soft 'plop' when you ran your palm over them, trapping them between palm and fabric, or between palm and skin, pressing down hard on their soft vulnerability, crushing them in irritated anger. They left a burning sensation on whichever part of your body they assaulted. And still more kept coming, buzzing and whining weirdly around your ears, getting on your nerves, driving you mad with impotent rage, for you knew full well you couldn't slam at the damn insects for fear that that might give you away. You never could tell – there might be somebody lurking just out of sight, planning to blow a few bullet holes through you, just to find out if you could bleed too. The mosquitoes kept coming at you just the same anyway, completely unaware of the fix you were in, flying weird, bloodthirsty sorties that made you feel light-headed and dizzy.

When the doves began to coo in their familiar throaty, soothing way, Apire crept up out of the swamp and headed south where, even in the twilight of nascent dawn, his eyes could sweep across a broad vista of almost bare landscape. On the far horizon were the vague rounded tips of a range of hills struggling to define themselves against the yielding gloom.

As he moved south, sometimes walking, sometimes running, sometimes hunkering down to reconnoitre, a lone shadow against a grey backdrop, he knew the war for him was over. He had made up his mind in the swamp while being assaulted by the infernal mosquitoes. The war was over for him: he knew he had lost the psychological mettle to fight on. He understood only too well the kind of bowel-wrenching fear that had gripped him as he had sped away from their attackers the previous day. That signalled only one thing - it was the end of the road for him. He had held life cheap before, other people's as well as his own, but now suddenly, very, very suddenly, the instinct of self-preservation had re-assserted itself. He would continue holding other people's life cheap, but not his own, not his own anymore. He wouldn't be able to lead any group of men into battle any longer, not with the cool bravado and reckless unconcern that had been his trademark before.

In any case, no sane man would henceforth be prepared to follow *him* into battle.

What tales was he going to tell about his exploits in the war? He chuckled as he remembered two of the stories that Lajaro the World War Two veteran had told him when he had been only about a metre tall.

He, Lajaro, had been made chauffeur to one of the British princesses because he was a 'terror' when it came to handling cars. Now there was this time he was driving 'his' princess – who sat reclining right behind him, for she simply adored the smell of his starched KAR khakis – in an open Rolls Royce, which was cruising at 180 miles per hour! Not even a Rolls being built to cope with that kind of speed, this one had disintegrated right in the middle of the road, sending them skidding along the road, still ensconced in their comfortable seats, he and his princess behind him. They had skidded for a few miles before coming to a grinding halt. Then he had turned round to look at the princess, who had promptly said:

'I love you, Lajaro' and he had responded by hugging her briefly and giving her two dainty kisses, one on either cheek.

Or the time he, Lajaro, and his team (he was football captain, you know) had been flown to Singapore in one of those huge planes which could carry all the inhabitants of a sizeable village on only one flight. In Singapore they were to play against another battalion. In addition to being captain, Lajaro was the best striker in his team. So good in fact that he didn't need boots in order to score. Just when the second half of the match had started, a team-mate had passed him the ball, which he had tapped skyward. But such was the strength of his leg that the ball had vanished beyond the clouds, giving him ample time to roll a cigarette and light it. When the ball had come down again, he had idly headed it into the net. And with his eyes closed too!

It was all very well telling such stories when you were an old World War Two veteran who most probably had never seen action, who could have been a cook or a dhobi, too busy ironing your officer's shirts and trousers and shorts and bedsheets and pillowcases to experience what it is like to be chased by screeching bullets and to spend a frightening night buried up to your neck in swamp water, with mosquitoes torturing you as if you'd committed a mortal sin. And when your injured arm all but hummed with pain.

Apire had decided he was going home. First to his mother, then to his ever-complaining wife. He knew Flo was right when she said his frequent long absences were eating away at whatever tenuous link still existed between them. True, he was taciturn and bad-tempered much of the time, but Flo would just have to continue putting up with that, for he had now realised that that was the part of his nature which nothing could change. He had come to like that aspect of his character less and less, but that was what he was at bedrock: a bitter, introverted, undemonstrative youth who would never be a good enough actor to dissemble effectively. He would never play the role of the buoyant, exuberant husband and father, nor succeed in scraping the imprint of bitterness and cynicism from his face.

He would, however, try to make his marriage work, if only for the sake of their son. But the problem with Flo was that she was too meek, too mild and almost acquiescent. If only she could assert herself occasionally!

***

Erabu was dead. Erabu, his constant companion for the better part of the war. Erabu, the ungainly young man with the protruberant eyes who had behaved like someone possessed by demons after killing his first man. He had run around camp alternately shrieking and cackling, leaping up in the air and landing in a heap like a sodden rag, ending up getting bruises all over his body and a bump on his forehead. But he had been disarmed, so he had not wreaked havoc among his comrades. For two days Erabu had been unable to eat. He had thrown up whenever he set eyes on fresh meat. His only sustenance had been roast cassava and water and *malwa* bought for him a few kilometres away from camp. Then suddenly he had recovered and become his usual cheerful self again.

And now he was dead.

Erabu, whom he had at first met by sheer coincidence.

Erabu, whose group had become integrated with theirs after a shoot-out that had left a few men wounded, but none dead, on either side.

Erabu, who had joined the war in the hope he would eventually get hold of a few cattle and go off to marry his Esina.

Apire walked among the short-stemmed cassava plants, his legs beginning to drag with weariness and his eyelids getting heavy with drowsiness. His stomach was beginning to growl and contract with hunger. He was feeling drained and dull and numb and top-heavy.

When he came upon the young man in tattered jeans and checked shirt, Apire recognised him at once. He was one of those who had survived the helicopter attack and the ambush afterwards. He had been having a bout of diarrhoea and Apire couldn't help wondering as to where he had found the strength to escape.

The young man was kneeling, the tips of his fingers planted like tines on either side of him and slightly forward to prop him up. He was bringing up floods of coagulated stuff that had the appearance and consistency of curdled milk mixed with green algae. He didn't seem to have any stomach at all. Beside him was an uprooted stalk of cassava with two tubers missing and in front of him were strewn cassava skins on which the streams of vomit occasionally splashed.

Apire walked over and gently touched his convulsed shoulders. If the man had been startled, he didn't show it. He looked vaguely up at Apire, and a weak, uncertain gleam of recognition came into his eyes.

'It's this – this – cassava – aa,' he stuttered, 'I ate it - a lot - poison.'

A jet of vomit streaked out of his mouth. Apire leapt back.

'One of us – wounded – bomb – that way.' His head swivelled to the right. He slumped forward and let go of another load of vomit.

Apire was bewildered and felt helpless. There wasn't anything he could do to help this young man who had fallen on hard times. He just stood there, watching him heave up diminishing loads of vomit, speaking incoherently in between, until he keeled over and landed partly on the right side of his body, partly on his face, part of his body coming to rest on the vomit. He lay still.

Apire knew the young man didn't have long to live. The cassava he had eaten was highly poisonous, and he must have been ravenously hungry to have eaten so much of it, for it was not palatable at all. He must also have had an exceptional kind of stamina, surviving so long after gorging himself on the bitter tubers.

Apire turned right and began walking away in the direction the dying man had indicated vaguely with his chin. He was beginning to feel feverish from the wound in his arm but when he saw Erabu, the nascent fever simply vanished. Erabu sat hunched up, his back against a tall dead tree that stood white and gaunt in the centre of a sorghum field. His arm was a mess from shoulder to elbow: shreds of flesh hung like a tattered garment over the shattered bone that poked out jagged and bloody at a crooked angle. Apire could see the yellow fat inside the bone. The flesh had turned a dirty green colour and there were fat flies crawling all over it; also worms moving in their obscene shortening and lengthening way. The arm stank!

Apire leant over Erabu, trying to fight down the gorge that was rising bitter and inexorable up his throat.

'Erabu,' he called, 'Erabu, it's me, Apire.'

Then the revolting sight and stench of the putrefying arm overpowered him and he threw up.

Some birds flitted twittering among the tall stalks of sorghum, perching on them and running up them to peck hurriedly at the ripe rich-yellow or brown clusters of grain at their tips. A vulture brooded on a high branch of the dead tree, sharp-eyed and slovenly like an old man in a shabby grey overcoat.

Apire had not noticed the bird before. Some vague feeling that he was being watched made him look up. He stared at the bird. The bird stared back, unflustered. Apire felt anger rising up his throat like a steel ball and choking him. He raised his gun, then realised it wouldn't do for him to draw attention to himself in this desolate place. He lowered the gun.

The vulture had left its perch on seeing the gun raised and moved to another tree a few metres away, flapping its wings lazily. When it landed, it manoeuvered itself into a position from which it could watch what was happening under the tree it had just left. It was now preening one wing.

'Erabu,' Apire called again. 'Erabu.'

Erabu didn't respond. Collecting himself, Apire moved closer and, placing his palm under Erabu's chin, gently raised the face so the eyes could look up directly at him. Erabu whimpered weakly.

Though Erabu was very dark, his skin colour had deepened to an almost blue-black shade. His head was bloated and the eyes were glazed with fever. Apire could feel the heat seeping into his hand as if from an oven. Erabu's breathing was very weak and laboured, but still one could feel the heat on his breath.

He didn't recognise Apire, didn't even seem to realise that there was someone right there in front of him, was completely unaware of his surroundings.

Apire withdrew his hand gently and Erabu's head sagged back on to his chest again. Saliva began to dribble from his mouth.

Apire took off his shirt and wrapped it around his shoulders, passing the left sleeve – which had been restored to its full length – around his mouth and nose to ward off the stench. He brought the cuff of the sleeve and the shirt tail together and tied them in a knot behind his left shoulder. Then he went off in search of leaves to use as a fly-whisk. He came back with a bunch of leaves and began fanning the mangled arm.

When Erabu finally died, late in the evening, he simply gave a weak sigh and toppled sideways. Apire stretched him out on his back, pressed his legs together, pushed his arms against his sides. Then he tore off one of his shirt sleeves and wrapped it around Erabu's head, knotting it at the back.

It wasn't easy breaking leafy branches with which to cover Erabu, for Apire's energy was depleted, partly by hunger and partly by tears left unshed, by deep imploding sorrow and anger that did not permit of a reinvigorating purging. Eventually, however, he succeeded in securing enough branches to completely cover his dead comrade and friend, tucking in some leaves along the sides.

He held sole vigil until the break of dawn, then he got up, weary and physically drained, and went his way.

X

'Where's Flo?' Apire asked his uncle.

'Gone off to see her folks,' answered the uncle.

'No,' replied Apire.

'At least that's what she told me. That she would be going to visit her folks.'

'And I am telling you that she's not with her people. She stayed with them for only three days.'

'How d'you know?'

'I asked around.'

'Then could she be with Maria?'

'No, she's not with Maria either. I saw Mum on my way here. She said it was two months since Flo had last paid a visit to her.'

'Then where could she be?'

'Only God knows. When did she leave?'

'Five days ago.'

'I see.'

'You don't look healthy. Unlike the first time you came back from that war.'

'This time it was different.'

'And your arm looks stiff. Your right arm.'

'Yes, that's why I say this time it's been different. I've been hurt.'

'Where?'

'On the upper arm.'

'Show me.'

Apire silently rolled up the long sleeve of the plaid shirt he wore, rolled it up to the shoulder to show his uncle the spot the bullet had grazed. The wound was a scabby furrow across the surface of the upper arm.

On his way home, Apire had dropped by a dispensary and told the Medical Assistant he found there that the bit of flesh missing from his arm had been gouged out by a nail. He had not explained how. The medical man had looked suspiciously at him, long and hard, and had asked for his ID card and money. He had produced both. Then he had been given an injection and some tablets and had left the dispensary.

There was nothing about Apire that suggested he was a fighter. He didn't have a military bearing. If one ignored the face, one would get the impression he was one of these contented, happy-go-lucky, exuberant people who are always smiling and laughing and patting others on the back. Especially now that he was not in uniform. He was clad in a plaid linen shirt and denim pants that he had stolen from a deserted homestead the same day he had walked away from Erabu's leaf-shrouded body. He had streaked across the backyard of the homestead from the nearby bushes where he had been hiding to wait for the people around the home to disperse. He had jerked the denim trousers and linen shirt off the clothes line and then had fled back to the bushes.

One thing that had helped him to get away was the fact that he had had only an old pair of trousers on – old and threadbare around the knees and the seat. He had rolled the trouser-legs past his knees so that, what with the old soot-covered palm-leaf bag that he carried, as well as his unkempt hair and the old plastic sandals on his feet, he had looked just like any other peasant going about his daily business. He had taken care to wrap the wound on his right arm with a rag.

He hadn't wanted to be asked a lot of questions, though, for despite his rather effective attempt at disguise, people had become exceedingly nervous and were apt to ask a stranger who he was, what he was, how come he was in their area and where he was headed to. To make it worse, there had been those stolen clothes in the bag together with the gun which he had dismantled and wrapped up in banana leaves like elongated pieces of meat.

He therefore hadn't followed any of the frequently used paths for fear he might meet exactly the type of people he was making an effort to avoid. He had been passing through an area where people like himself were not appreciated in the least, so he had avoided his fellow human beings as best he could. He had also wanted to put as great a distance as possible between himself and the place he had stolen the clothes from, but without running, much as he felt an almost irrepressible urge to do just that.

Fortunately for Apire, he had the kind of nose which could smell a human presence from miles away, so he had found it easy to avoid people. If where he hid there was an anthill, he would go behind it, let down his trousers and go through the motions of relieving himself. Now, in case he had been spotted rushing off out of sight, whoever would have wanted to investigate would have been too embarrassed to ask even a single question on finding him crouched in that revulsive position.

When he had felt he had walked far enough to be safe, he had climbed up a leafy tree on a farm and settled himself in the crotch between two branches. He had eaten some boiled potatoes and raw white ants which he had stolen from another home that same day. He had felt thirsty but had thought it wasn't safe to get down from the tree to look for water to drink. That could wait till nightfall. In any case, the few people he had met on his way to the farm, whose sudden appearance had made his bowels loosen, his bladder convulse and his heart flutter, were enough for the day. He had felt a stupefying drowsiness draw over him like a canvas sheet and, though he had tried hard to fight it, he had eventually fallen prey to the seductive pull of sleep. When he had woken up later, much, much later, wondering how he had managed to hang onto the tree in sleep, he had climbed down and got into the stolen clothes, leaving the trousers he had been wearing under the tree.

'You had better quit that silly war,' Apire's uncle said.

'I have come home, Uncle,' Apire said.

'You have come home in order to rest a little and then go back.'

'I have come home to stay,'

'Promise me you will stay home and look after your son and your wife.'

'Well, where's my son?'

'With his grandmother. Sleeping.' 'Grandmother' was Apire's uncle's wife, Pulu.

'And Apire?'

'Yes.'

'Your wife has been looking sad, except of late. You had better make a real effort to make her happiness last.'

'I will try.'

'Really work at it. Try to make up for the many long moments you have been away.'

'I will try, Uncle.'

'I am glad to hear that. Now I shall wake up Pulu to get you something to eat.'

'No, I don't feel like eating anything.'

He didn't want his uncle's wife woken up because he secretly feared her unsparing candour, her often caustic tongue. He was certain by the time she got round to bringing his supper – if that was what one could call it – she would have given him a piece of her mind regarding his frequent disappearances and his neglect of his wife. She loved Flo and deeply hated the war.

His uncle reached up above the stack of split firewood arranged carefully on a supporting rack of more firewood stuck endwise in the empty space between the top of the wall and the roof thatch. He lifted down an old lidded enamel bowl that was deep and discoloured by soot, for its resting place was directly above the fireplace. He placed the bowl beside his stool and then took down a chunk of roasted cassava.

'You will at least eat this,' he said.

'And what is that in the bowl?'

'Simsim paste.'

'Oh.'

'Will you eat it?'

'Let me try.' Apire felt relieved and eager, but he didn't want to show his eagerness after having prevented his uncle from waking up Pulu. The uncle removed the lid and gouged out a dollop of simsim paste, and another, and yet another with his fingers, spreading the paste thick and brown and glistening on the cassava. Then he handed it to Apire.

Apire gratefully accepted the cassava and bit into it. It felt soft and powdery and melded easily with the paste to form a yielding ball of mellow fragrance in his mouth. He ate in silence as his uncle resumed his pipe-smoking, ruminative.

When he finished eating, he dipped up a calabash of water from the big waterpot stationed beside the door and drank it. It was only then that his uncle spoke.

'I am going to bed," he said.

'Well, I think it is time we retired for the night.'

'Sleep well, son.'

'Sleep peacefully, Uncle.'

The two had been talking in the smoke-filled kitchen. Apire's uncle usually took his time over a pipe before going to bed in another grass-thatched hut which served as both living and sleeping quarters. Pulu hated the smell of fresh tobacco smoke and always insisted the uncle smoke his pipe outside when she was in the kitchen, and anywhere else when she was in the other hut. She seemed, however, to find the stale smell of tobacco tolerable, for she hadn't yet gone to the extent of banishing her spouse from the conjugal bed, which she always shared with him, and often with Apire's son as well.

Apire had turned up that night, deliberately at a late hour, only half expecting his uncle, whose nocturnal habits he knew very well, to be still awake. He had walked stealthily up to the kitchen door and looked in through the crack between door and doorjamb and watched his uncle smoking for some time. He had looked serene, contemplative and ascetic and strangely disembodied in front of the dancing flames of the log fire that had thrown his shadow convulsing and jumping frantically against the arc of ash-smeared wall behind him. He had called his uncle by name, his voice a barely audible whisper. His uncle had looked up, startled.

'It's me, Apire,' he had said, louder this time.

'Oh it's you,' the uncle had said, sounding not surprised at all. He had got up slowly from his cane stool and walked over to the door and removed the long threshing-stick with which he always propped the door shut.

When Apire's uncle had bidden him goodnight, Apire had proceeded to his own mud-and-wattle hut beyond that in which the uncle slept, but he couldn't sleep. His heart kept fluttering and thumping in an unaccustomed way the whole night. A vague suspicion kept plaguing his mind, something inchoate and nebulous that didn't seem able to coalesce into anything concrete, anything tangible. It made his head ache and eyes smart even in the inky darkness, it kept pressing in on him, inexorable, never really letting go for one single moment, so that he felt boxed in, felt a heavy, choking restlessness about him that was oppressive like the narrow confines and stuffy air of a water-soaked dungeon.

He also felt betrayed – how he couldn't tell. He believed a husband should always find his wife where he had left her when he returned from his wanderings. At least, that was what a loyal wife should do. She shouldn't go off on errands of her own the moment the husband's back was turned. Now what was he going to do? Just sit around day after day to await her return? And what was he going to do with their boy with whom he always felt so awkward whenever the two of them were left to themselves? That boy whom he loved more than he had ever loved anyone but to whom his demonstrations of affection had never gone beyond the occasional gentle pat on the head and pinch on the cheek and the pancakes and biscuits and sweets and bananas that he sometimes brought home with him from his drinking places? That boy who always looked at him with that accusing and reproachful something in his oh-so-much-like-Flo's eyes? He hoped the boy wouldn't turn out like him – bitter and cynical and hurtfully sarcastic and often despondent...

But where was Flo? What was the logic behind her telling his uncle that she would be staying with her parents the whole time she was away – at least what she said implied that much – and then just vanishing like that? No, he wasn't going to sit on his bum like an idiot and wait for her return. Come morning, he would begin his search. He would look for her until he found her, even if it meant going to her parents and giving them a little shakedown. He knew of parents who actively encouraged their daughters to elope with other men if they felt that the daughters were getting a raw deal from their husbands, as Flo's parents most probably felt she was. Such parents usually had their sons-in-law beaten up by their younger clansmen, especially their own sons if they had any; or if you didn't take a thorough bashing, it was your mother-in-law herself who broke your head with a pestle. And if you said you wanted your bridewealth back since your wife was now living openly with another man, then the repayment would be spread over a lot of years: a cow and a few shillings one year, a hen and two hoes during the second year, nothing during the third, then perhaps a goat and a spear blade in the fourth...

Well, he would go to them just the same, anyway, and ask them whether they were aware that their daughter had developed the capacity to make herself invisible and see how they liked that!

He kept tossing in bed. He would lie on his belly one moment, squeeze his eyes shut in an effort to induce sleep, fail, turn onto his side, try the same trick again, fail, roll onto his back, stare emptily up at the unrelieved darkness for some time, shut the eyes tight, fail to woo sleep, open them again.

And the hours moved thick, slow and heavy like syrup. At the second cockcrow his thoughts turned to the possibility that now as he lay half-nude and cold and alone, somebody could be sleeping with Flo, his Flo; and in his mind's eye he saw every detail of that intimate act and it made him want to get up and begin looking for Flo that very moment. He tried to block the thoughts from his mind but they only receded for a few moments and came spilling back, more oppressive and aggressive than before, washing every other thought out of their way. He felt an unfamiliar burning sensation behind his eyeballs and knew he was close to tears. Then the tears began spilling down his cheeks, at first rolling in slow beads, then suddenly turning into two hot salty trickles. He took a long time weeping, shedding tears of self-pity and wondering all that time, why are you pitying yourself you fool you've only just survived a war in which you lost a dear friend and you didn't weep for him and now you arrive home and begin spilling tears like an old man and all because of a woman's thing!

When dawn broke, his eyes felt as if a sheet of sandpaper had been drawn across them. He had been in that twilight world of half-wakefulness and half-sleep, that limbo state of neither-nor, with the senses dulled yet never soothed, sluggish yet aware of sounds and smells and the feel of the bedclothes and the heat behind the eyes and the shame of having wept like an old woman approaching senility; he had been in that state since the third cockcrow.

When Pulu knocked on his door, he lay listless and unmoving and continued staring up at the part of the roof where the central pole connected with the thatch.

'Open up. It's me Pulu,' she said. Her voice sounded muffled from the early-morning mist that came swirling into his hut, mist that was fine and gray and wafted in wraithlike and held you in its chilly embrace. He wondered why Pulu should have decided to see him at such a time, risking a bout of illness since she was asthmatic. He drew his trousers on over the brief pants under the pink bedsheet, zipped up the trousers, got up and began walking towards the door.

'Apire, are you listening?'

'Yes.'

'Then what are you still keeping to your bed for? There is something important I want to tell you before going to the well.'

'I am already here, Pulu,' said Apire as he flung the door open.

When Pulu entered, she closed the door and settled into one of the two chairs in the hut - a rather crudely-made folding affair that had become brown and smooth with use. She silently motioned towards the bed, and Apire moved backward and sat on it.

'Apire, I have had a very bad dream,' she said, without preamble. She sounded strangely subdued, and even in the semi-darkness of the hut's interior, he thought she looked quite sad. 'I dreamt that Flo and your son were hurtling down a fast-flowing river in a dugout canoe. Only the two of them were in the canoe so there was no one to row it for them. Flo was trying to get away from you, taking your son with her. As the canoe sped down the river, entirely at the mercy of the currents, it tossed violently hither and thither, and all the time Flo was screaming abuse at you, at all of us, screaming at the top of her voice, telling the whole world she didn't care a damn what happened to her and her son, she was bored sick of you, of us, all she wanted was to get away, away, get away before she became insane, either get away or die. And the kind of language she was using! I haven't heard fouler language in my life. Then the bottom of the canoe scraped over a huge rock which had suddenly loomed in their path and the canoe was ripped in two. They were flung into the river clutching each other and she still screaming abuse. They went down together but kept coming up after that, tens of times, each time getting farther and farther down the river, and each time, too, Flo's voice getting less frantic, gentler, and a happy smile bathing her face the last time they came up, as if she was happy to die. Then they drowned."

'My god, what a dream!'

Apire didn't believe in all that mystical stuff about dreams having the capacity to foretell events, but this one chilled him just the same.

He frequently had his scaring dreams, and they were often more frightening than the one Pulu had only just narrated; but they were usually about events that had actually happened, things that he had witnessed himself or that he had done, about people dead and dying with eyes and heads exploding and bodies getting chopped into minced meat and flesh putrefying and fat flies sucking greedily at the sickening sticky juice, but these were not dreams which touched his living family, his mother and sister and brother and uncle and aunt and son and wife. They were remote dreams that occasionally assumed a surrealistic form, only rarely appearing like past events viewed through the distorting angularity of a prism.

Now here was this dream about his wife and son going off in a canoe like a couple of crazy people and their boat getting dashed against a rock and both of them perishing in the depths of some river gone mad with lust for human flesh and blood. He didn't like the dream, didn't like it at all!

'Now what do you want me to make of the dream?' Apire asked.

'Well, I know you young people of today do not think dreams are important. When we were young, if you were preparing for a journey and you dreamt that something bad happened to you or a close relative and you didn't sneeze on waking up in the morning, you simply put off that journey.'

'What do you make of that dream?'

'I didn't sneeze when I awoke, so don't go back to that war.'

'I told Uncle last night that I wasn't thinking of going back to the war.'

'He told me. But I want you to promise me too.'

'I won't go back to the war.'

'Say "I promise".'

'I promise.'

'That's good.'

'It might be good, but I still don't quite see what that dream has to do with my wishing to go back to the war or not.'

'Mmm,' Pulu said, looking steadily at Apire. 'Mmm. You are a man now, Apire, not the little boy whose bottom I used to wipe with green leaves whenever you came to visit us. Being a man means having a heart that can bear a lot of pain. I am an aging woman who may not be having long to live, what with this *asima* which neither our traditional herbs nor the white man's medicines have succeeded in curing. When my time comes to depart from this earth, I would feel that my life has been worthwhile if I left you happy.'

Apire wondered what all this was leading to but didn't interrupt.

'Apire.'

'Yes.'

'I have always loved you, right from the time you were a little boy running around naked and unashamed with snot plugging your nose. I have loved you despite your being a very difficult child to understand, despite your never being able to talk much, to reveal your innermost thoughts, despite your looking sad most of the time. You are to me more of a son than you will ever be to anybody else, not even Maria. Maria has her other children, but I have only you whom God has had the kindness to send along to replace my three children who were killed in early infancy by jealous neighbours, leaving me childless to date. Are you listening Apire?'

'Yes, I am listening, Pulu.'

'Do something about Flo.'

So this is it, thought Apire.

'Well, I have come home, and as I told you, I am not going anywhere now.' There was an edge of irritation to his voice.

'Apire, my husband told me during the night that you had found out Flo was neither with her folks nor with your mother. Do you have an idea where she is?'

'No, Pulu. I wanted to try and find out today. Is Uncle's bicycle in good condition?'

'Yes, but the bicycle wouldn't help you much. Some of the menfolk around here would be of greater use to you than the bicycle.'

Apire's heart skipped a beat.

'What do you mean about the menfolk being of greater use?'

'Apire, I am a woman, and as a woman I hear a lot of things that do not get to the ears of men. Us women, we have plenty of secrets which we often do not tell you men, for fear you might react very violently. Remember that while you are busy drinking, we women are most times gathered somewhere, around the well, or in a neighbour's house doing each other's hair, or in the bushes looking for firewood, and gossiping all the while.'

'And what have you been gossiping about?'

'"Who" would be better.'

'Who have you been gossiping about?'

'Flo – Flo and the Catholic priest. The choir practice she goes to has more to do with her admiration for the priest than with singing. There actually seems to be something raging between them. Now in case she is with the priest, your male friends could help you arrest them.'

'That-that-p-priest,' Apire stammered, clenching his fists, 'I will...'

'Before you will do anything, I want you to know one thing, Apire. What I have told you about Flo is only gossip, gossip that has been going around the village for some time now. The rumour seems to have originated from among those nuns who appear to be more jealous of the priest than if he were their husband. So it is just possible the nuns put that rumour about out of spite since the priest had been giving a lot more attention to Flo - perhaps strictly as a member of the church choir - than to them.'

'Who gave the son-of-a-bitch the bloody right to give my wife such attention?' Apire bawled. His heart was racing now and he felt like getting up and doing something drastic, but his knees felt weak and shaky like a rickety camp chair.

'You did, Apire,' said Pulu, firmly yet gently.

'I did what?' Apire exploded.

'When you go off somewhere leaving your only blanket spread out on the grass and it gets beaten by rain, you have only yourself to blame if you have to cover yourself with a wet blanket at night.'

'Flo is no blanket left out in the rain. You were there to look after her and keep her company. And there was our son to keep her busy and talk to her when you were away?'

'Apire, I think you are still very innocent. A woman needs more than protection and somebody to talk to. She needs a man, a real man to keep her warm and busy most nights. Certainly you haven't been that kind of man for long periods at a time. So when Flo begins casting about for somebody to make her feel like a woman, I find it difficult to blame her.'

'So you connived – you never really wanted Flo to continue being my wife, you collaborated with her so she could trip off to that worthless priest and – oh my God, I have been betrayed!'

'Don't be silly, Apire, and sit back down. What do you think we are, a couple of wizards? We have watched closely over Flo, and that is why we have discovered so much about her. But she is not a child. She is a mature woman who has the right to a certain amount of freedom. What did you expect us to do to her - keep her chained hand and foot to the central pole of your hut each time we went somewhere?'

'But you could – you could have talked to her – warned her about the dangers of such behaviour – how it can make a man feel cheap – a laughing stock. You could have warned off the priest – told him to mind his church duties and to stop fooling around with people's wives.'

'Apire, we talked to Flo. We asked her whether it was true what was being said about her and the priest. She said there wasn't any truth in it at all. But we warned her just the same. We told her she was cheapening herself sleeping with the priest – if it was true she had been doing it – that married life meant patience and forbearance and always taking full advantage of your man when he is around and turning your thoughts to other things when he is away, things like farmwork and making mats and minding your child and assisting other women instead of traipsing off to choir practice the moment the priest called. She told us nobody was going to stop her attending choir practice since that was the only diversion she had.'

'It's not like her, being so defiant.'

'She's changed a lot. You will notice it the moment she comes back. There is something about her that I haven't noticed before, something that reminds me of a woman contented and fulfilled.'

'I will not notice anything of the kind about her. I will be too busy beating her to notice how contented and fulfilled she looks. I will beat her, thrash her till she craps on herself and then I will send her packing to her parents. Then I will see to that priest.'

'Instead of "beating her, beating her" in your head until she shits all over herself, you should be thinking of doing a little research around the mission. Somebody is bound to know if she is there. And if she is there, get some people to arrest her and that priest boyfriend of hers.'

She got up. 'Now, I am going to the well.' She opened the door and departed, leaving it ajar.

Oh Flo, my Flo going off to get laid by a priest as if she weren't married. Now wherever I go people are going to take one look at me and think there's something wrong with me, otherwise why would my wife do a thing like that? What a hero's welcome for a man who almost left his skin in a war that now seemed so distant, distant and faint like the peal from the tall belfry of a faraway cathedral on a cold, misty morning, a war that had left him feeling neither like a victor nor a loser. It was just a war like many other wars that left you feeling lost and flat and weary and more grown up than your agemates, but also a little more cowardly, though in a more brassy, loudmouthed way, wanting to prove to yourself all the time that you've quit the war with your bravery intact and undented.

Where had he seen an inn called Horizontal Hotel? At the time, he had wondered what abysmal lack of imagination could have made someone name his hotel 'Horizontal', but now it dawned on him that perhaps the person who had done the naming had the sort of impish imagination that was denied the rest of mankind, an imagination that unravelled lots of implications in even such a plain and ordinary, know-a-little-arithmetic word as 'horizontal'. For didn't a hotel always have a set of rooms to hire and wasn't it true that people often went to those rooms in twos, both during the day and at night, and when in the rooms they became horizontal? There was certainly some logic in the naming of that hotel, though at first it had struck him as singularly, absurdly inane. And now what was he going to do if he discovered that the priest – what was his name, Wila, Dila? well, he would find out in due course – had been 'going horizontal' with Flo all the time he had been away at war?

Oh stupid young man, you've been betrayed. You war-hero that's no hero stealing other people's clothes and hiding behind bushes and slogging home only to find out a priest has been flattening out your wife and giving her regular infusions of the man-seed that the frequency of your absences from the marital bed denied her. You're a proud man, Apire, why are tears springing to your eyes? Haven't you always said – asserted in fact – that women were just like surgical gloves which should only be appreciated when still in the pristine state, fresh and unsullied by contact with ailing human flesh, and should be discarded at once when they became soiled, contaminated? What are you going to do about your wife who's turned adulteress after only four years of marriage, you strutting, short-legged young cock?

Burn her with your cockscomb? Why are you pitying yourself, shedding silent tears like a cripple when you have your gun and twenty rounds of ammunition that you could use to wake up the night and send a few more people packing to the Kingdom of God?

Apire wept. Apire wept more than he had done during the night when he had had the grudging suspicion that something had gone seriously wrong with the relationship between him and his wife. Now the nascent suspicion had found a name, adultery, and he liked it even less. Sorrow wrenched at his soul and the tears came spilling out drenching his cheeks and spattering the floor in front of his bed as he sat on the bed with his palms cradling his chin and cheeks and wept. He was still weeping when Pulu came back from the long walk to the distant well and looked in and nodded her understanding and commiseration and moved quietly away. The tears were still sweeping down his face when his son turned up to check who had opened the door of their hut so early in the morning and came bounding in calling 'Mummy, mummy, mummy' and then, realising it wasn't mummy but daddy, asked: 'Daddy, why are you crying? Has Grandfather beaten you?' and hovering around his knees a moment, curiously watching him, with something impish and disdainful about his face, and then skipping off to announce to Pulu: "Grandmother, Daddy is crying" and Pulu replying "He's unhappy" and a long question-and-answer session following upon that. Apire wept silently, choking down the sobs that kept rising up his throat, wept until his eyes felt sore and his head ached and his body felt drained and weak and discomfitingly weightless. Then he went looking for his gun which he had hidden in a bush a few metres behind his hut.

* * *

It was night and very dark. Apire moved cautiously, watching for moving shadows and hiding behind anything that could afford a cover the moment he spotted anything coming his way whose manner of movement or shape was even remotely human. His AK47 with the folding stock was thrust down under the waistband and inside a leg of his stolen jeans, the steel of the gun coldly stinging his right thigh. He had removed the magazine and rammed it into one of the numerous pockets of the jeans. It was late at night and he knew that not many people would be about at that time of night, and the few who were would be those returning from a bout of drinking who wouldn't be able to distinguish any shape at all from far off. Apire was headed for the Catholic Mission.

Apire had kept to his hut the whole day, venturing out only when there was urgent need to do so, because he had not wanted any of the priest's friends to see him and rush off to report his presence to the padre. If the priest came to know about his being around, Apire was sure he would instantly smuggle Flo out of the Mission. If she was with the priest, that is, something his mind readily accepted the probability of but that his heart kept hoping was not possible. He knew that in any clandestine affair involving a housewife, there were always confidants of the philanderer who kept on feeding him with information that made it possible for him to avoid traps set by the cuckolded husband. If the husband was aware, that is, as he had brutally been made aware by Pulu. Only this was no trap he had set, but a trap that the priest had set for himself.

Pulu had not wanted Apire's son to disturb his father so she had induced him to follow her wherever she went by constantly plying him with simsim paste and roast white ants and boiled sweet potatoes, so the little boy had trailed her the whole day, failing to see why he should go to a father who had been crying so early in the morning when his "grandmother" had so much that was nice to eat to give him. And Pulu had ensured that her cornucopia lasted the whole day by drawing on it at carefully-spaced intervals.

The priest kept some foreign breed of dog that was tawny, shaggy, big and fierce and had the sharp-snouted look of a fox. Apire clecided he would try as much as possible to avoid a showdown with the dog; but if he couldn't avoid an encounter with it, then he would decide what to do when they came face to face.

He ambled past the gate and continued walking along the barbed wire boundary fence. He turned a corner of the fence and crawled under the bottom strand into the banana grove beside the Nuns' Home. Now, it's going to be a bit tricky moving from here to the Mission House, Apire told himself as he tugged the gun up and out, fished out the magazine and rammed it home. He released the safety catch, cocked the gun and headed for the Mission House.

His heart had begun to thump and a certain dryness engulfed it, making it feel dessicated. The thumping of the heart almost suffocated him, so that he felt light-headed and groggy. He saw a faint light filtering through a blue curtain in one of the glass windows and hurried towards it thinking, this should be the bedroom, otherwise what would he be doing in any other room at this time of the night? He heard the dog barking around the catechumens' sleeping quarters and knew he wouldn't need to do anything about the dog after all, probably it was barking at a catechumen come out to pee and that would keep it busy for some time. He became bolder and crashed past a rose bush whose thorns clawed at the sleeve of his shirt and he jerked it irritably away.

When Apire arrived at the lighted window, he felt giddy and in his ears was the wild pounding of his heart so that at first he couldn't hear anything else. Then he heard it, as if in a dream, it came barging through the din in his ears, faint but overpowering and piercing his heart, and making his head spin, so that he just stood there gulping for air like a fish run aground, gulping down air and trembling violently and getting weak at the knees and wet at the eyes. Yet the squeaking of the bed and the sighing and sobbing and slapping sound went on and on and on and on. And he still kept on feeling like a man struck with a mallet on the back of the head, standing there gaping and blank and with eyes shut wetly tight, fighting despair, subconsciously trying to shut out the reality that was in there, just beyond that lighted window, trying to obliterate the indestructible, the abomination that was being committed on his wife at that very moment.

Light-years later, Apire recovered his wits and began feeling more stable on his legs, and still the sounds of secret pleasure kept hitting him, but they no longer made him dizzy. Instead he felt an incandescent rage building up inside him, the kind of rage he had felt at the battlefront, an intoxicating lust for blood. The gun came up, mechanically, the hands moving it up as if they were acting independently of the rest of the body, responding to an in-built will of their own; the gun went up and the barrel angled downwards and the muzzle pointed at the spot where the sighing and sobbing and giggling were coming from. Then a steady finger squeezed the trigger, slow and sure, and the gun spat a trail of streaking flame that shattered the window and raised a few piercing screams where there had been only pleasurable moaning and protesting and grunting. The bullets streaked raw and incandescent and unbroken, shattering the deceptive peace of night. When the bullets stopped ripping, there was no sound coming from inside the Mission House, nor was there any sound outside the window apart from Apire's laboured breathing. And there was the smell of cordite swelling around the window and the rose bush like an aftertaste of doom.

Apire spat, turned and left.

* * *

Apire walked throughout the rest of the night; and when morning came, he was still trudging along. He felt a feverish determination to reach the police station before midday. He was hungry but his legs were firm. He carried the gun in the same sooty bag in which he had carried it in bits and pieces a few days before. This time he had not bothered to dismantle it.

Apire arrived at the station at around eleven and found a bored corporal sitting with his elbows planted on the top of the long desk in Reception, his chin supported between his palms. Without preamble, he took the magazine out of the bag and put it next to the corporal's left elbow. The corporal sat up and raised his eyebrows, inquisitive. When the gun came out, held dangling by the folding stock in front of the police officer's nose, the cop sat petrified, wondering whether he wasn't in the presence of some nut escaped from a mental home and whether he shouldn't raise the alarm to seek assistance. But at that moment Apire spoke, still holding the gun like a pendulum.

'This gun is empty,' he said. The officer wanted to speak, to ask what business it was of his to be requested to look at a gun that was empty, but his voice failed him. 'This empty gun,' Apire continued, 'has committed a crime. It has killed a priest and my wife. Well, anyway, I think they're both dead because when I left, neither of them was talking. That is why the gun and the magazine are both empty. They did their work.'

If the policeman had only been suspicious before, now he was sure that this man with the sleep-starved and opaque eyes was mad. Yet there was no dancing light of madness, no frenzied stare, in those eyes! What on earth had he done to be saddled before lunch with someone who definitely was speeding down the slipway to absolute insanity? Now he was going to lose his appetite!

When Apire placed the gun clattering on the desk top, the policeman leaped up, eyes wide with fear, and began backing towards the wall behind him.

'Hey, Officer,' Apire said, 'there's nothing to fear. I'm not mad, if that is what you think. I'm here only to report a crime I committed last night, you hear?'

'What the hell do you mean a crime you committed ?' the cop, finding his voice at last, bawled.

'I told you, didn't I? I killed a man and a woman last night. My wife and her boyfriend. I caught them in the act. I want to make a statement.'

'I am *not* going to take a statement from someone who might be demented for all I know!'

'Then you may lock me up and go off to investigate.'

A sergeant poked his head through the doorway behind the corporal. 'Abdalla, what's the matter?' the sergeant asked.

'Look at that desk! This man here walks in and places a gun and a magazine on top of the desk and tells me not a single bullet is left in either. Then he claims he's shot two people dead and asks to be allowed to make a statement. Or locked up. I think he's a mental case, sir.'

'I am not a mental case, sergeant. I am only trying to save you the trouble you'd have been put to trying to track me down if I'd decided to run away. Or go into hiding.'

The sergeant took a step inside Reception.

Are you serious about the claim you're making here?' he asked.

'I'm in earnest, sergeant.'

'And you are aware that murder is a very serious offence which might earn you a life sentence or a hanging?'

'I'm aware but I don't care either way.'

The sergeant fixed him with a long, cold stare.

'You're mad,' he said, finally. 'Corporal, take down his statement.' Then he turned and left.

The corporal resumed his seat and began to fire away. Apire answered the questions as best he could. When they were finished, the corporal asked him to hold out his hands so he could be handcuffed. He obliged almost eagerly. Then he was led to a cell and locked up.

Epilogue

The Daily Chronicle, Thursday 14 September.

'Murderer' gives himself up

At 11.00 a.m. today, a young man reported at the Pataka central police station and claimed that he had killed a Catholic priest and his lawful wife the previous night when he had caught them making love in the mission house. He produced an AK47 sub-machine gun that was not loaded and an empty magazine, which he said constitute the murder weapon, to substantiate his claim.

Francis Apire, 25, a former driver-mechanic and rebel who hails from Atari village in East Pataka district, looked haggard and subdued and was unwilling to talk when this reporter visited him in his cell.

Besides affirming that the self-confessed "criminal" made a statement, the police were not forthcoming with more information about him, asserting that they still needed to verify the information that Apire had supplied them with.

The Daily Chronicle, Friday 15 September.

Rebel kills adulterous priest – confirmed

Police yesterday afternoon were directed to the scene of a double murder committed by a young man, one Francis Apire, 25, who had reported at the Pataka central police station earlier in the day and produced the murder weapon, an AK47 sub-machine gun.

When police and Apire arrived in a British aid Landrover, registration number PP 0126, at the scene of the crime, a rural Catholic mission situated two kilometres east of Atari trading centre, they found a big crowd gathered on the mission grounds and some people, including the chief catechist, were in the priest's bedroom. The bodies of the victims of the murder, a youthful Father Santo Dila who returned from a course of study in Italy two years ago, and the murderer's wife, Flo, were in the bedroom. The priest, who had been shot through the heart and had bled profusely, was lying on his back on the only bed in the room while Mrs. Apire lay in a pool of her own blood on the floor. She had been shot several times, with four bullets lodging in her body and a few more inflicting minor injuries. They were both naked.

The motive for the murder is believed to have been jealousy. Apire seems to have gone to the mission to investigate his wife's whereabouts and found her and the priest making love.

On-the-spot post mortem examinations revealed that the two had died as a result of extensive damage to their internal organs as well as haemorrhage.

When this reporter asked some of the local people to comment on the incident, their general opinion seems to have been that both Apire and the priest were at fault, the former for frequently neglecting his wife for long periods of time and the latter for getting involved with a married woman. One of the people asked suggested Catholic priests should be allowed to marry in an attempt to ensure such embarrassing incidents do not continue to occur.

Glossary

adere	*malwa* drunk straight from a receptacle, preferably without recourse to a sucking tube
Afande	way of addressing one's superior officers in the armed forces
asima	vernacular equivalent of 'asthma'
askari	here, local administration policeman
atap	millet bread
chapati	food made from dough rolled thin, flat and circular and baked or fried in a shallow pan
gomesi	traditional dress for women among some ethnic in Uganda
kanzu	here, cassock
kiboko	whip or cane
kitenge	printed material for women
kwete	a mild alcoholic beverage prepared from maize, with millet or sorghum yeast
mabati	corrugated galvanised iron sheets
malwa	a popular drink made from maize or millet, sorghum
Mulokole	(plural, Balokole:) born-again Christian
ngwara	method of felling a person by kicking both his feet away from under him
ogwang-gweno	same as *askari* above
olam	a tree with a spreading crown and very sticky sap
opobo	a plant often used as a whip by parents
poo	a black-and-yellow hardwood
sigiri	a kind of brazier which uses charcoal
sufuria	aluminium saucepan without a handle
ugali	bread prepared by stirring maize, millet or sorghum flour in boiling water until it sets into a fairly firm ball

Wandugu   (singular, Ndugu) Brothers.
waragi   a crude gin

Python, oh python
Don't break my chest
Oh python!

Python, oh python
Don't break my chest
Oh python!

Rup rup rup rup
Don't break my back
Oh python!

Rip rip rip rip
Don't break my back
Oh python! *

* Translation of song on p.45.